His Rules
BDSM Erotic Fantasy

Written by Tiny Sparks

AF351281

Author's note

Unlike the BDSM Erotic Stories series, this series is pure fantasy. Some of the scenes are possible, other's are just fun. Safety and aftercare are included in these scenes, but the scenarios can be a bit out there.
Therefore, please keep it safe, sane, and consensual in real life!
Now, without further ado: enjoy this fantasy!

Chapter One

I entered my favorite pub, and sighed in relief upon seeing Klara and Georgia waving me over. My face ached with the strained smile I had kept in place, but once they stood up and hugged me, I couldn't hold on anymore. The tears flowed freely.

"Sweetie, It's all right. Deep breaths," Klara said patting my back.

"Yeah, Greta, we're here for you. You don't need to worry," Georgia chimed in.

I grabbed a tissue from my jacket. They cringed as I loudly blew my nose.

"What?" I sniffed.

"Not very ladylike, hon." Klare raised an eyebrow.

"Screw you, Klara, I don't feel like being a lady when my boyfriend of three years fucks me over with his secretary."

My friends held their hands up and took their seats. I draped my jacket over the back of my chair and tried to wave over the waiter.

"So, what's the plan now that you're officially single again?" Georgia asked.

"Found an apartment this morning. It's nothing much, but I can afford it for a little while until I get a job." I shrugged.

I'd been a trophy wife of sorts. Even though we hadn't been married, he wanted me to stay home. We'd even had a maid come in twice a week, meaning no house work for me. Staying home doing absolutely nothing was maddening. He wanted me to maintain a certain image, which he thought was perfect for a promotion at work.

I'd been good at it too. A couple of weeks ago, when I went to surprise him with a meticulously prepared lunch, I found him banging his secretary.

Honestly, I wasn't surprised. After three years, we only had sex once a week, on Saturday. I'd stopped trying to reach an orgasm. I just let him get it over with.

"You know, my sex life with that loser was lame. I need to get laid properly," I said, surprising both my friends and the waiter who had just stopped at our table. Realizing he'd heard me, my face flamed. I ordered chicken wings and the café's signature ice-cream, hiding my embarrassment behind the menu.

When Kara raised an eyebrow at me, I stuck my tongue out. Now that I didn't need to keep up the image of being perfect, I was going to eat whatever I wanted. So what if I gained a few pounds? If a man didn't find me attractive, that would be his problem.

"Well, I can't help you with the sex part, or your questionable food choices, but I can help you on the job front," Kara offered.

"Thanks." I ducked my head.

"What do you mean 'lame'?" Georgia wasn't one to keep her mouth shut when it came to sex talk. Me? I wasn't so open, normally. However, when the waiter came over with shots, probably ordered by Kara, I downed three in a row. That loosened me right up.

"Always missionary. I mean he did try to do foreplay, but I wanted more and when I mentioned it, he'd look at me as if I'd grown horns." I gazed into the last shot glass.

"More?" Georgia prompted.

"I don't know. Holding my hands above my head, maybe? Taking me by surprise from behind, blindfolding me?" I surprised myself by mentioning all that.

"You know, next week is the BDSM party. It might be on the more extreme side of what you're mentioning, but why not come along and see if something catches your interest?"

Georgia and her husband Ty were into leather and BDSM. I didn't know what BDSM entailed exactly. She'd been trying to get me to come along to one of the casual meetings for ages, but my ex had never been a fan of them. Since he was out of the picture now, I could hang out with whomever I wanted.

"Yes! Come on, Greta! I'm going, but I'll be the third wheel if you don't come along!" Klara had gone twice and both times had come back with stories that made my panties wet.

Should I? Why the hell not?

"Okay! It's not like I have anything else to do." I shrugged.

The girls cheered, and we threw back another shot. The chicken wings arrived just as my stomach rumbled.

Aside from the booze and wings I had one more sin to complete this evening. The giant ice cream, which you normally ordered to share, I polished off all by myself, to the surprise of the waiter. There were six scoops of various flavored ice-creams, nuts, chocolate crunchy bits, caramel, and a giant dollop of whipped cream. It hit the right spot every time. And it had been three years since I indulged.

I could tell Klara and Georgia wanted some, but they knew better than to get in between me and my creamy comfort food.

Chapter Two

Klara forced me to wear the only mini skirt I owned, and gave me fishnet stockings and a fishnet top under which I had to wear a red bra. I tried to pull the skirt down to cover more of myself. Then I saw what she was wearing, and felt better. She wore panties and shoes and nothing else.

She laughed when she saw my expression. "Don't worry, you'll see stranger things."

We covered ourselves with a long coat, and left with an Uber. Once we arrived, I gaped. It was a warehouse.

"Are you sure this is the right address?" I watched Klara saunter to the entrance and open the heavy metal door. There wasn't anything to see beyond. It was pitch-black. I fastened my pace to make sure I didn't lose her. Light filtered through a second door. If I didn't know something was here, I'd never have entered this place. It was in an industrial area to begin with. But I guessed that was the whole point.

"Sean, how are you?" Klara kissed the guy who opened the door.

He was a head taller than me and built like a bodybuilder. Maybe he was the bouncer, even though he was dressed in black chaps and a collar in matching leather. He turned around and I blushed bright red. His ass was bare. It was a nicely rounded muscled ass, but still, it was bare.

"Eyes up here, young lady."

I gazed up barely escaping whiplash. His grin was followed by Klara's laughter when we went deeper into the warehouse.

My eyes adjusted to the dim light provided by a few windows higher up, and some spotlights. The floor was concrete, but the furniture was luxurious. Leather sofas were scattered around the huge area. In between the sofas stood wooden benches, with chains attached to the floor and the ceiling, which was at least sixteen feet high. Wooden crosses were situated randomly against walls. Some surrounded by chairs, others on their own.

Two crosses were occupied, of which one by the only couple I knew.

I smiled and waved at Georgia. My smile wavered when I saw what she was doing. Her grin was pure pleasure when she stroked her husband's red bare ass. She was covered from head to toe in a lycra body-suit. The high heels of her boots could kill someone, or in my case break an ankle. He was naked except for a shiny collar. His hands and ankles were attached to the cross with cuffs.

She held a black riding crop, which she rhythmically tapped against her leg. Since she was busy, I checked out the rest of the room and found the bar. Ordering a drink, I turned on the barstool and took in the activities. One couple in particular caught my interest.

The woman was splayed over the man's lap. Each slap of his hand made her butt jiggle. Her face was flushed, and her head shot up when he made contact. In between hits, he stroked her bottom which she tried to lift it. Squirming on the barstool, I imagined myself over his lap. When his fingers disappeared between her ass cheeks, and her mouth formed a perfect 'O', I was sure she was coming. However, the rhythm of his pounding hand between her legs increased. When his other hand squeezed around her throat, she went rigid. I thought she was choking, until he let go and she quivered all over. He lifted her off his lap. She trembled on her legs, and he grabbed a blanket in which he enveloped her before sitting down with her in his arms.

Averting my gaze I caught another scene. Here a guy in costume was binding a woman with rope. The intricate patterns were mesmerizing and when he motioned someone on the side, she was lifted off the floor. All the knots and ropes were connected to a ring which rose closer to the ceiling. She hung sideways, one leg bent and her arms behind her back. It didn't look comfortable and when he pulled on one piece of rope her bend leg went higher, opening her legs as wide as they could under a protesting groan from the lady. He moved closer, supporting the bend leg on his chest. He opened his trousers and pushed his cock inside her. The woman was immobile but for her head which she threw back moaning loudly.

I gulped down the glass of chardonnay I'd ordered, and got up. I found Klara bound against one of the crosses, being whipped. I watched for a few minutes and sought out the bathroom. I needed release and soon. Sitting down, I dropped my panties and leaned back against the toilet seat. I closed my eyes when my fingers found their way to my wet pussy. After coating them with my juices, I circled my clit, and thought back to the girl being slapped and Klara being whipped. It didn't take long for my breathing to shorten and my pussy to pulse. I rubbed faster. My stomach grew tight and my legs clenched and unclenched against my hand. I barely held back the moan trying to escape, as I reached my orgasm. A few aftershocks later, I slumped on the toilet seat with a grin. Humming from the orgasm, I washed my hands.

When I joined a now blushing Klara and a smiling Georgia with her husband at her feet, I listened to their idle chatting. Klara was ready to leave after half an hour. She had to work the next day. Half a day of which she promised to use to look for a job for me.

Chapter Three

I'd checked my phone six times already, making sure the battery was charged since I didn't want to miss this call. The temp agency had sent me to at least eight interviews in the last four weeks, and none of them had panned out. The landlord had given me a two months' notice last week to either get out or pay. The two months was my deposit therefore he was in his legal rights to throw me out. The stingy asshole had turned off the heat of the water boiler. He claimed it was broken, but I knew better. The cold showers had been a harsh wake-up call. I needed this last job to work out. The pay was amazing, and I had a good feeling about the interview.

When my phone rang, I nearly dropped it. The screen was broken but it worked, another collision with the floor would mean the death of it.

"Hello?" I was out of breath, and my heart beat a mile an hour.

"Greta?"

"Kara! Please tell me you're calling with good news?"

"You've got the job! There is one issue, but I've decided to let it slide just for you."

"What is it?" Now I dreaded what she was talking about.

"They want you to sign the contract directly with them. Normally I wouldn't do that, but if you agree, then I'm happy to take the bribe they gave me, just don't tell anyone." She was laughing on the other side of the phone. Was she going crazy? Why would she joke about a bribe?

"Are you joking?" I honestly couldn't tell.

"No, I'm not joking. Well, I'm kinda joking. You see, this company is registered exclusively with me on condition that they pay me a large sum if I find the right candidate. The catch being that you sign the contract there. I haven't had any complaints yet. Two guys and one girl working in different departments were hired through me in the last two years. You'll meet the girl tomorrow. She works in human resources and will hand you your contract!"

"Tomorrow?"

"Yes, they want you to start immediately! Isn't that amazing?" A bell sounded in the background. "I've got to go, Greta, and good luck on the new job, I'll text you the address!"

Sinking down on my tattered sofa, I stared ahead. Did this really just happen?

"Yes!" I jumped up and danced around my small apartment. The thumping of Mrs. Dyna's broom in the apartment under mine didn't stop me from dancing. I did stop jumping up and down, though.

A text message came through, and for a second I dreaded it was Kara to say that the company called to cancel the interview.

It was the time and address for tomorrow's interview. Grimacing, I realized I'd need to take the tube, and that the trip would take me half an hour. That was not counting the walk to the station from my flat.

I'd be able to pay my rent, decent food and clothes and shoes. Dreaming away, I was slow dancing with my phone without any music.

A FEW WEEKS LATER, I was the personal assistant to Allan, the boss of the entire floor.

Allan called me into his office for a debrief. He had important clients coming in tomorrow and wanted everything to be perfect.

He's sizzling hot. Jet black hair slicked back, always dressed in a suit perfectly tailored to fit his wide chest and match those penetrating blue eyes. Even though it wasn't done to seduce your boss at work, it didn't stop me from wearing short skirts and opening one button too much. Unfortunately, all to no avail.

As his secretary, I am, therefore, not a possible partner. Every other day you hear about some sexual harassment charge in the news, so it's understandable that he wouldn't act on my signals.

Deep down I knew, the chances I was going to get laid by my boss were slim. Still, a girl can fantasize, right? I hadn't had sex in ages, and it was torture every day, watching him stroll around the office in those form fitting suits. I went home dripping wet every night.

"Greta, are you paying attention?"

Nope, I wasn't.

"Yes, Mr. Devon." I looked up at him.

His smirk made it clear he knew I hadn't been paying attention.

I hid my face behind my hair and started to write something down on the notebook I was supposed to take notes in.

"Greta, if you can't take notes, what are you doing here?" Allan sounded impatient.

Tapping my pen, I thought of an excuse for not listening that he might accept.

"I need to go to the ladies room." His raised eyebrows showed his doubt, but he let it go.

"Fine, we'll continue in a bit," he sighed.

Loosening his tie, he got out of his chair and stretched. The movement highlighted his wide chest and tempered waist. He was built like a football player. I swallowed hard, my mouth dried, and my pussy pulsed before I shook myself out of my daze. Bathroom. Right.

I passed an empty workspace. All the offices were empty. Checking the time, I realized it was after six. Bloody hell, I hated going home in the dark. It wasn't the first time he'd kept me late. Irritation made me hurry. He might be gorgeous, but he could be seriously annoying at times.

In the bathroom, I splashed my face to get the redness to fade. I'd never been this unprofessional. Sure, I'd flirted, but he never seemed to notice. Of course, my form of flirtation was smiling and leaving my blouse unfastened one more button than was decent. Probably why I had such a hard time getting laid. I was horrible at teasing and foreplay, I would rather just get to the action.

The door of the bathroom opened, and before I could gasp, a hand covered my mouth.

Chapter Four

"**G**reta," a voice I was intimately familiar with growled in my ear, "Not paying attention when I say something is bad form."

I nodded, excited and scared.

"You've been a bad girl, Greta, and I've finally figured out what I can do about that."

My eyes grew wide at the smirk on his face in the mirror.

"Do you agree that you've been a bad girl?"

I nodded again, my mouth going dry.

"So, when I let go, you won't scream?"

I shook my head. He shifted closer, trapping me against the sink before slowly lowering his hand.

"You've been offering me quite a few peeks of your cleavage the last few weeks. Now is the time to show me." It wasn't a question.

The pressure of his cock against my backside intensified, and his eyes locked onto mine in the mirror. They blazed with lust but seemed to give me the option of backing out. When I didn't do anything straight away, he closed his eyes and let out a frustrated sigh.

"Sorry, you didn't..." He opened his eyes, and they widened when I slipped the first button free. His arms captured me when he gripped the side of the sink. He pressed in closer and I couldn't swallow the moan.

I opened my white blouse further and was glad I had worn a sexy front clasp bra today. It was white lace with a red trim. A red little bow covered the clasp.

His gaze traveled to my breasts and a groan rumbled through his chest tightening my nipples. He just stood there watching me. I felt powerful, even though he had me captured within the circle of his arms. I could seduce him with an upper-body striptease. He swelled against my lower back. His arousal gave me courage to continue. I clenched my legs together where heat and moisture gathered.

I opened the cups and freed my breasts. Still, he didn't move his hands. He did, however, dip his head and lick my shoulder. I hummed. When he kissed my shoulder, it encouraged me to cup my breasts. I pinched the nipples and moaned, hanging my head against his collarbone. I pleasured my breasts and imagined his big hands on them.

His presence disappeared, and I opened my eyes.

Our gazes caught in the mirror. He undid his tie and raised an eyebrow in question when he shifted closer again. He held it before my mouth and whispered in my ear, "I'm going to need to gag you. The janitor has started his rounds, and I will be fucking you until you scream into my tie. Do you want to continue?"

Did I want to continue? Hell, yeah, bring it on! I moaned, rubbing my backside into his crotch and nodded.

He smiled. Like a good girl, I opened my mouth and let my boss gag me with his expensive tie. It would soon be covered in my saliva, but he tied it securely behind my head anyway.

His cock pressed against my bottom and wiggled a bit. This earned a chuckle but no action. He brought his hands to the front of my body. He shuffled forward as well, pushing my pubic bone into the sink. When his hands enveloped my breasts and pushed them together, I moaned.

"Hush now, or the janitor will hear you," he whispered in my ear.

His voice, his hands on my breasts and the knowledge that someone could walk into the bathroom any minute made me totally wet. I was so hot I was sure I'd combust at the tiniest touch on my clit.

He let the tap run on cold. One finger dipped in the water and he touched my nipple. My knees buckled at the contact.

I didn't need any touching of my clit, because I just went over the cliff in one swift swoop. Breathing deeply, I swished my hair back over my shoulder. His smug smile reflected my way from the mirror.

I swallowed the drool trying to escape from between my lips. Behind me, he slipped his hands under my skirt. I straightened, wanting his full body in contact with mine. I needed it, but he stood up straighter and held my wrists in his larger hands. Placing my palms on either side of the mirror arched my back and lifted my ass higher. My breasts dangled, and the slightest movement would bring one of them into contact with the still running cold water.

With my palms flat against the wall, I had to spread my legs apart to make sure I wouldn't slip. He rubbed the inside of my thighs. Up and down. My legs trembled when his touch went higher with each upward rub.

In one sudden move, he straightened, leaned over me, and licked my ear while he pulled up my skirt with one hand, slipping the other into my panties from behind. My skirt was around my hips, and his fingers were getting soaked with my juices. He took out one finger and sniffed it, then with a wicked grin he rubbed his finger over my lower lip. His big hand grabbed my chin and roughly twisted my head to the side. He licked my juices off of my lower lip before letting go again.

Now moving fast he opened his trousers, ripped open a condom package and expertly fit it onto his rock hard cock. Then he shoved my panties aside and entered me in one swift thrust. I couldn't hold back the groan. He grabbed my hair in one hand and held my back down with the other.

Damn, I loved it rough. I wasn't sure if I was going to be able to stay quiet for long.

Little whimpers escaped me, and he grabbed onto my hips, slamming into my pussy harder with each thrust. Out of the corner of my eyes, I caught a glimpse of movement. I stiffened immediately.

Chapter Five

"Damn, woman, you're tight and hot as hell," Allan growled behind me.

The door to the bathroom opened and my eyes widened when I saw it was the janitor. He wasn't just watching, no, his cock was out and his fist was tightly wrapped around it, moving in time with my boss's thrusts. The pervert was jerking off. I wasn't sure if I was grossed out or fascinated. I couldn't stop watching his thick fingers stroke his long cock. He looked bigger than Allan. This random man was getting off on me getting manhandled by the big boss.

I tried to catch Allan's eyes to warn him. I grunted, but he didn't quit his pounding. He grabbed on to his tie and my neck snapped back so far I couldn't see anything but the ceiling. I closed my eyes and imagined what the janitor was watching. I was getting a thorough fucking from behind, with the tips of my fingers barely touching the wall. My breasts were swaying with every thrust. Allan fisted his tie in one hand and stroked a path to my left nipple with the other. He pinched it, and my legs started to shake with the impending orgasm. My inner walls squeezed his cock hard, and he couldn't hold on any longer. One final push, and he pulsed inside me, giving the correct contact of his balls to my clit to take me over the edge. Delicious aftershocks of my orgasm continued as he thrust a few more times.

When he let go of the tie, I looked at the door. The janitor was nowhere to be found. I sighed in relief.

The boss tucked himself away, and with a bright smile, patted my ass affectionately.

"Make sure to get that tie dry cleaned, all right. And wear something sexy tomorrow." With that bit of information, he left.

Why did I have to wear something sexy tomorrow?

"Not much of a gentleman that one, huh. Suit could've fooled ya, but then again..." the janitor snickered.

Upon seeing him, I fled into the stall nearest to me. I buried my head in my hands.

How could I be turned on by knowing he'd caught us?

I haphazardly put myself back together but beyond adjusting my clothes, wasn't sure what to do. As for what had just happened, I couldn't call it sexual harassment since I enjoyed it. When I came to work tomorrow, I wasn't sure if I could look Allan in the eyes. If I gattered the courage to come back. And now this janitor was out there and had seen it all. Had he taken pictures?

I groaned, holding my palms to my burning cheeks.

Chapter Six

"You know, he's done this before. Did you read your contract in detail before signing it?"

Huh? What did he mean by that?

"He's used to getting his way with his secretaries. And there is a clause in the contract that states that he is within his rights. You stupid women are always blindsided by his charms."

I opened the door to the toilet stall and opened my mouth. He moved fast for an older guy and clapped his gloved hand over my mouth before I could scream.

"That contract even states that every employee and client can have his or her way with you."

I shook my head in disbelief. No way could I have overlooked such a weird clause.

"He always gets the first turn, so the lot of us had to wait quite a while. I don't know what it is about you that had him waiting for such a long time." His hands smelled like chlorine.

Waited? I've been working here for barely three weeks.

He'd turned me around, and I was with my back against the sink. The same sink that the boss had bent me over only a few minutes ago. Even though he was older than Allan, he wasn't bad to look at. And that cock I'd seen him massaging earlier was impressive to say the least. It pressed against my tummy, and I couldn't stop imagining him taking me with his dirty cock. Some moisture escaped my pussy. My panties weren't in the right place yet, and my wetness slipped past my pussy lips down my legs.

"Ah, well, I get seconds and am happy about it!"

Gleefully, he picked me up and threw me over his shoulder. I was too dazed to do anything. He was damn strong and carried me like I weighed nothing more than a rag doll.

Slapping me on my butt, he said: "Let's have some fun, little bitch. Be glad he took you first. You might have noticed that I'm a bit bigger than him. So hopefully, you're still a bit stretched from his cock."

Dear Lord, I couldn't stop the humming. My body was preparing itself for the next round, and my mind was trying to catch up. I tried to see where we were going but hanging upside down wasn't giving me many options to check things out.

"Here we are," he said as he opened the door.

Chapter Seven

I t was the janitor's closet. It had a small table in the middle, on top of which he dropped me. Leering at my helpless state, he made quick work of unbuttoning my blouse again. I couldn't help the intake of breath as his gaze of appreciation roamed freely over my bare chest. He took off his gloves and proceeded to give my breasts more attention than Allan had given them before. He was gentler but firm. His hands were slightly callused and large. They enveloped my breasts completely, grazing my sensitive nipples with his palms. I put my hands over his and encouraged him to squeeze a bit more. He complied, and I sighed in contentment.

When his hands disappeared, I pouted and pushed myself up on my elbows. He'd gone down on his knees and started to lick and kiss my thighs. He shuffled closer to my pussy and my attention seeking clit. Then the familiar whine of a lowering zipper spiked a fresh wave of heat through me. Closing my eyes, I imagined him stroking himself while his mouth neared my slit. His two-day-old beard and mustache were deliciously grazing my sensitive thighs. When he zeroed in on my slit and pushed his tongue inside me, his mustache touched my clit, and I nearly jumped off the table at the sensation.

Holy crap, I almost came right then and there from a mustache.

I panted as he worked his mouth around and his mustache touched my clit again before he flicked his tongue fast and hard. I shattered.

He didn't waste a minute. Grinning, he positioned himself at my entrance. In one smooth thrust, he entered me. My eyes widened when I heard him grunt. I looked to where he thrust a second time and realised I'd taken most of his cock but not all. I was so full already. I wasn't sure I could take more.

He was so big, I was getting a bit worried. I tried to shift up a bit but he grabbed me around the throat and started thrusting for real. He looked me deep in the eyes, and that was always a huge turn on for me. Then he flicked my clit with his thumb lightly in a steady rhythm. I moaned loudly, biting my lip to try and keep the shouts from escaping. His hand moved to my mouth. He went balls deep slow stroke after stroke. Thr rough palm left my clit and he leaned over me, never taking his eyes from mine. When he encouraged my left leg to lift, I screamed in his hand. He was in to deep and it hurt with each thrust. I grabbed his hand and tried to take it off my mouth.

"Too deep?" he asked. I nodded.

With a grunt he stood and pushed my legs down. His thrusts increased in speed, but they didn't go as deep. His hands free again he pinched my clit, which sent me into a shaking orgasm. With a final thrust, he went too deep, but my orgasm didn't stop at the pain, it increased. Just as I was about to scream again, he covered my mouth and stayed burried diep, lying on top of me. His elbows lifted his weight. I kept spasming around him and he stayed still letting my orgasm finish before removing his hand and himself.

When the janitor let go of me, I slid to the floor.

"You okay, honey?" He almost seemed concerned.

It's a bit late to ask.

My body was limp with satisfaction, and while maybe I should have been upset and offended, I wasn't. I nodded at the nameless janitor.

"You should probably check your contract, because I'd love to enjoy more of you." The smirk was on his face again. After the satisfaction he'd just given me, it no longer annoyed me.

Lifting me up, he kissed me hard. I couldn't say anything, still too stunned from two hard fucks and the news of my contract. He helped me getting my clothes right, as my hands still shook.

Chapter Eight

I walked to Allan's office. Taking a deep breath, I pounded on the door.

"What?" he asked in an exasperated voice.

When I enterd he asked: "Greta, why are you still here?"

"Is it true what he said?" I asked in a small, quiet voice.

"What?" He seemed utterly confused.

"That I signed a contract giving you rights over my body?"

"Yes and no." He ran his fingers through his hair.

"What does that mean?" I almost yelled, in frustration.

"That maybe, you should have read the contract before signing it," he snapped. "Sorry, but you are the second girl that didn't read the contract apparently and still had sex with me." He sighed.

Did he have no clue how hot he was? It didn't surprise me that I wasn't the only one.

"What does the contract state?" I asked, curious now about what I'd supposedly agreed to.

He got up and riffled through some papers in his desk drawer.

"If you aren't in accord with what it says then please rip it up and leave. I do believe HR made it clear to read the whole thing before signing?"

I nodded because they had pressured me into reading it before signing it. The first page was very similar to that of my previous job, and I'd just paragraphed all the other papers and signed at the bottom. I needed the money to be able to pay rent and have electricity, so I hadn't bothered to read the rest.

He left the office without saying anything. I started reading. Halfway through there was indeed a clause that stipulated sexual contact. It was quite clear that by signing the contract, I agreed to have sex with anyone the director of the company deemed in need of sexual release. There was also an open paragraph on the bottom of the page that asked to specify the acts that I would not agree to. If the paragraph was left open, it would be up to the director (Allan), to decide for me.

I bit my bottom lip. I'd enjoyed having sex with the boss and the janitor but this meant having sex with anyone he wanted me to have sex with. How could I still be considering this? Was I going nuts? I should rip this up and quit on the spot.

Just as I was about to toss the whole thing in the bin, my phone pinged.

'If you want to talk the contract over, come to the following address.'

Talking about it never hurt anyone, right?

It made me wet just thinking about going to his place, so why did I hesitate? Maybe because the man wanted to make me into a prostitute with the salary of a well-paid secretary and still do the work of a secretary on top. I could take his contract straight to the authorities, and they'd put him away and throw away the key. Probably. I had signed it, after all.

Then there was the fact that I still needed the money and couldn't afford to get fired straight away. Maybe I could work something out temporarily. A probationary period or something.

I took an Uber to the address he'd texted and read through the contract again on the way. There was an open paragraph that stipulated if left blank, anything goes. What the hell did that even mean? Did that mean things like piss and shit included? Cause I was so not into that stuff. I guessed I was going to have a very embarrassing conversation with my boss.

Ringing the bell, my hands started to sweat. When a buzzer indicated the door was open, I entered a rather lavish looking hallway.

Plush carpet led the way to one door, so I walked over and opened it. There was a huge living area, decorated in a mix of Victorian and modern styles. Leather red chairs surrounded a dark heavy oak table. A Chesterfield sofa dominated a place in front of a silent TV and crackling fireplace.

Allan sat on the sofa with his legs crossed, one arm over the back of the sofa and one hand holding a glass of wine. He had taken his jacket off and lounged in his blue dress pants and half unbuttoned white shirt.

Like a scared mouse, I stayed in the doorway. The whole scene was both inviting and terrifying.

"So, you've decided not to quit, I see," he said pointing with his glass to the contract I was fiddling with.

I opened my mouth but nothing came out, so I nodded.

"Close the door, please, and take a seat," he ordered.

Shaking with nerves and excitement, I followed his direction, sitting across from him.

"Now, the field you left blank, I'm pretty sure it was unintentional and will need it filled out by tomorrow, do you understand?"

Again, I nodded and opened the contract. I cleared my throat and forced out the question that had been playing on my mind.

"What exactly do I need to fill out?" It came out as a hoarse whisper.

Raising an eyebrow, he lounged back and sipped his wine. My suddenly dry throat longed for a glass.

"It asks about your boundaries," he said.

I nodded again, still staring at the page.

"An easy one is, anal, yes or no or want to try."

I gaped. The smug bastard winked at me. He knew I'd never done this before and was making fun of me. Cheeks hot and pissed off, I stood.

"Fine, I will have it on your desk by tomorrow morning." When I turned around to leave, he halted me.

"I need to know a few things before tomorrow as I won't have time to read it by the time the clients arrive."

I slowly turned around. "What do you need to know?"

"Threesome, DP, female, anal, consent."

My mouth opened and closed a few times before I took a deep breath. "Yes, unsure, yes, unsure and what?"

"Do you give your full consent to wear our product and have sex with my clients if they wish it tomorrow?" He raised an eyebrow and took another sip of his wine.

How could he converse about this so casually? And what product?

"What product? And I have to choose now?" My hands were on the verge of crumpling the contract.

"The product is a body cream which you will demonstrate, and yes, you have to choose now." He kept eye contact.

I was tempted to break it, but lifted my chin. "Are your clients aware I am not a whore?"

"They are aware that you consented to do this as part of your job as my personal assistant and secretary."

I didn't know when they started calling a whore a personal assistant.

"You will get a bonus if the clients are happy and invest in the product. One thousand dollars to be exact."

I tried to keep my mouth from dropping open but couldn't. I didn't think a prostitute gets paid that much money.

"Okay, I give my consent."

"Very well, I'll see you tomorrow." His smile didn't reach his eyes. I guess having to pay someone extra to do what was in the contract they signed wasn't something he was happy with.

But I didn't care, I was going to get paid to be pleasured. Hopefully the clients were not fat or ugly. I've always fantasized about pleasuring a woman, and now I was going to get to do it. I didn't feel like a whore, strangely enough. With a happy skip in my step, I hailed a cab and went home. I was going to need my beauty sleep.

Tomorrow was going to be very interesting.

Chapter Nine

I woke up early, feeling more refreshed then I had in a long time. I grinned as I remembered how satisfying yesterday's actions were. A beep had me jumping out of bed and heading straight for the shower. I didn't want to be late.

Allan wanted me to find something sexy to wear? Shit. I didn't have anything. That's what living on my meager income had done. My closet was bare, what little I had was on the bed, and the sexiest thing I owned was the pencil skirt and white blouse that I wore the day before. I'd thrown away every item I'd ever worn when I left my ex.

Yesterday's outfit would be it. Makeup, shoes, jacket, and I was on my way to work.

"Greta, get in here, please!" Allan yelled from his office. I hadn't even taken my coat off or put my handbag away.

Opening my coat, I checked my blouse making sure I undid an extra button before I entered his office.

"Go through that door," he pointed to the left, "and put on the clothes that are lying there, after applying the cream to your entire body."

I'm not sure what I expected, but to be dismissed wasn't it. I opened and closed my mouth.

"Something the matter?" With an irritated sigh, he lifted his head to glare at me.

I shook my head and hurried over to the door, my heels clattering on the ceramic floor.

Walking through, it was as if I'd entered an alternative universe. The door closed softly behind me. Inside, dim red light illuminated a room out of my biggest, baddest fantasy. Fantasy being the operative word.

The walls were padded in black leather with a plush red love seat placed in the middle of the room. One wall was decorated with all sorts of sex toys, dresses, cuffs with and without fur, leashes, a multitude of leather whips, dildos and vibrators in various sizes, and butt plugs.

I didn't have time to inspect it all too closely since he'd told me to change.

Across the room, a black silk curtain covered the dressing room. I tiptoed closer to a stool sitting in front of a mirror with a makeup table. A long, white dress hung on the wall next to it. There was a huge assortment of eye shadows, pencils, lipsticks, and anything else I might need to go crazy with my inner makeup artist.

A white plastic pot dominated the middle of the table. On the lid were simply instructions: 'apply all over, inside and out'. Frowning, I tried to figure out what that meant.

Well, with all the sex toys, maybe I had to smear it in my pussy. I certainly wasn't putting it in my mouth.

Shrugging, I undressed and searched for a place to put my clothes. Underneath the table was a small cupboard, perfect to store my purse, underwear, and clothes.

Checking out my nude body in the oversized mirror, I was quite happy that even though my breasts were large, they didn't sag. My dark nipples stood at attention with the cool air caressing them. My stomach was flattish with a slight rounding ending in my venus hill. My gaze followed my hand. I grimaced when I noticed how red everything was. Shaving all over the day before had sounded like a good idea yesterday.

I grabbed the cream and started applying it. The silky feeling calmed my sensitive skin. I slathered it all over my body. Shaking my long hair out of the tight professional bun I'd had it in, I let it fall in a wave of blond curls down my back.

A beep followed by Allan's voice, made me jump.

"Greta put on the dress. I'll be with you in a minute. And drink some water, please," the clear sound of his voice made me wonder if he was spying somehow.

When I slipped the seemingly modest dress over my head, I noticed straight away that it wasn't designed to be modest.

A deep V neck in the front came down to my belly button, and the scraps of cloth barely covered my breasts. An elastic kept the waist tight, while the length of the dress flowed with extra fabric. The sides had long peek-a-boo slits in the fabric, barely covering my butt or pussy. No underwear was provided, so I went without.

The door to the office opened and Allan, my boss, strolled in. Inhaling his spicy, masculine scent as he entered, I closed my eyes for a second, enjoying it.

His broad shoulders nicely filled out the black suit he was wearing, and he stalked toward me with the confidence of a tiger about to pounce. I wasn't short or thin by any standard but I felt petite in his presence, something I relished. He closed and locked the door behind him, making me swallow my now dry throat. Grabbing the bottle of water, I twisted the cap off, and took a large gulp.

"Bend over the love seat, please," his command rumbled through the room and straight to my clit.

I gladly did as he asked, peering over my shoulder as he approached, his footsteps muffled on the thick carpet.

"Face forward."

My cheeks flushed as I obeyed.

His large hands caressed my butt as he brushed the silky fabric of the dress aside. Cool air caressed my exposed behind, and I bit back a moan. His thumbs slipped between my butt cheeks and pulled them apart.

"There isn't enough cream applied here," he murmured. I hadn't paid much attention to the amount of cream I'd rubbed into my skin.

His hands traveled lower to my pussy, and pushed down on it with the heel of his palm. This time I couldn't stop the moan from escaping.

He chuckled a low rumble. "There's enough cream here," he said.

I hid my head in my hands, and groaned.

"Stay here," he commanded and gave my ass a light smack.

I shivered at the loss of his warmth. Allowing him to control me to this extent, excited and scared me.

When he came back, he opened my crack and applied more cream. The tip of his finger massaged my rosebud and even ventured a tiny bit inside. I groaned when he pushed in further.

"A bit tight here, we'll have to see about loosening you up later," he commented.

Next, he applied the cream to my clit, and I nearly jumped out of my skin.

"Sh, it's okay, just some extra cream." He caressed my thighs and butt with one hand, relaxing me again. "Stand up and turn around."

Confused, I did as I was told. He wasn't going to fuck me? I swallowed my disappointment and faced him.

"Hands behind your back," his graveled voice commanded.

With one finger he caressed the fabric of the dress aside, baring my nipple so he could apply more cream. However this cream wasn't white like the one I used earlier, it was translucent. He repeated the process on the other nipple. Putting the fabric back into place, my nipples poked through the white fabric where the cream or gel had made the white almost see-through.

Grabbing my chin between his thumb and forefinger, he tipped my head back, forcing me to meet his gaze.

"Now, we're going to go into the next room where I have two very important clients waiting to check out the brand new product," he said, his voice husky. "There are two products. Remember, you agreed to stay quiet and do what I and the clients request at all times, right?"

I searched his eyes and didn't see any compassion which worried me. I'd gone this far, and now all I could think about was getting fucked. My skin was aching to be touched, and my clit was painful and rigid. My body was screaming for satisfaction, especially after feeling his hands stroke me. Not to mention, this room brought every fantasy I'd ever had about submission and sex to life.

"Yes, Sir," I replied without hesitation.

The widening of his eyes pleased me to no end. He stroked my cheek and kissed me hard. I wanted to wrap myself around him but he'd already let go.

"You get one word. Use it only when absolutely sure. This word will not get you fired, it will not get you in trouble. It will only get you sent out of the room for the remainder of the discussions and sales pitch." His gaze laser focused on mine.

"Apple," I said loud and clear, understanding perfectly what this was all about.

The room we were currently in and my research over the years, gave me that much of a clue at least of what to expect. I had this strange desire to not have to use the word. To not disappoint this gorgeous man in front of me.

"Good, let's go."

He took my hand, and we walked to a door I hadn't seen before. It was a part of the leather covering. All I could think was 'thank god' because I was pretty sure the other office workers were as clueless as I had been about what was behind door number two.

Chapter Ten

We entered a room decorated as both a boardroom and a restaurant. A large table with chairs around it dominated the room. Next to it was a smaller, more elegant table with a white cloth, wine glasses, and even a candle. A giant of a man inspected the three cylinders displayed there. He wore a black suit with a red shirt and a black tie. The tie was loose around his neck, and his jacket hung open. He stood between the table and a wooden contraption with a leather padded top.

I'd seen those before online when I was searching for porn, and it was similar to a restraining bench.

"Good afternoon, Mr. Reesly, and welcome to my special office." Allan greeted the giant.

I stayed near the door, shivering with anticipation, as Allan strode forward and shook his hand. The man didn't move, but let his gaze rest on me. A smirk appeared on his lips.

"The comparison, I presume?" he asked, nodding in my direction.

"Greta, come over here, please," Allan commanded, irritation clear in his voice.

I padded over eagerly on bare feet.

Allan guided me towards the contraption. He came behind me and pushed me forward, so my front ended up on the padding, my breasts dangling on each side. He lifted my hips, which put my pussy on the edge, and me balancing on the tips of my toes.

"I trust you've had a chance to fully examine the products I sent?" Allan said to the client.

"I have, Allen, and I'm ready to see if it lives up to its promises," the big man leered at me as he answered my boss in his cheerful, upper-crust British accent. "I thought that I would fit on the cylinders first and then compare them straight away to the subject."

His wicked grin made me realize that I was the subject in question. While they were talking to each other, Allan fit cuffs on my wrists and ankles and attached them to the bottom of the wooden structure. When I tugged at them, I couldn't move. Allan turned my head to the side so I could see the table and the man standing next to it.

"Are you comfortable?" Allan whispered close to my ear, his warm breath tickling my neck.

I nodded. As if he couldn't stop himself from touching me while I was helpless, his hands roamed the length of my back. Bending over me, his fingers skimmed down my arms. I moaned as his hard cock pressed through his trousers against the bare skin of my vagina. When he disappeared, I whimpered in disappointment, only to moan again when his hands cupped my ass cheeks, pinching the sensitive skin. He squeezed them and slid his hands down my legs to my ankles. He'd succeeded in making me a quivering mess with a wet pussy ready for penetration. For some reason, my nipples were heating up and cooling down as was my clit.

Allan circled the table and sat down, inviting the client to share a glass of wine. He poured himself one and started a conversation with the leering man. I only caught a word here and there. Pussy and cock sleeve. Spanish fly droplets in water.

The sudden pulsing sensation in my nipples and clit had all my attention. I gasped, my eyes widening. I was on the verge of an orgasm without being touched. I couldn't relax since the orgasm didn't reach its conclusion, leaving me on the verge of satisfaction without actually getting it. Sweat beaded on my upper lip.

"Please," I begged.

The conversation stopped.

Allan frowned but the other guy laughed.

"I guess it's time to see if your product lives up to the real thing. It's a pretty little thing but I don't need to see her face or her breasts since I'm supposed to use my imagination with the cock sleeve." The guy stood up and took off his jacket. He came closer to me.

"You'll enjoy this as much as I will, I'm sure," the guy whispered in my ear before covering my upper body with his jacket. A belt rattled as he untied his, and then a zip of his zipper.

Allan was going to let this guy fuck me, and I couldn't care less as long as he was going to make me come.

"I'm not a fan of the mouth cylinder, I already know that." The jacket muffled his voice.

"Okay, so it's just the cunt and ass you want to compare to the sleeves?" Allan asked.

"Yes."

"She's tight in the ass as she hasn't had one in there yet, as far as I know."

I stiffened at this comment.

"The sleeve wasn't too tight that I couldn't enter it, so the feeling should be similar."

A hand caressed my ass, fingers moving the cheeks apart and something wet dripped on my hole.

"You made the sleeve to accommodate me personally? Are there plans for different sizes?" He was still talking to Allan while rubbing the lube, I presumed, with his thumb over my ass hole. My hips gyrated on the bench, trying to move his fingers where I really wanted them; my clit.

"I hadn't thought about that, as the cylinder sleeves give way for every size. The silicone is treated to allow it to get pushed aside, similar to vaginal muscles."

When the tip of his thumb entered me, I groaned.

"She's tight, all right," he commented while rotating his thumb.

He took his thumb out, and I relaxed. More lube was added, and he slipped two fingers inside easily before I tensed up again.

"Ah, that's a good girl, relax and just take it," his voice was not as dominating as Allan's, but it still commanded compliance.

He twisted his fingers, and I tried to relax as much as possible.

"That's the good part of the sleeves, you don't need to put in the work. You can just fuck them," Allan said. His voice sounded amused.

"Very true, but then it doesn't moan and squirm either," the voice behind me answered distractedly. Allan hummed in agreement.

"Might be something I can figure out in the future. To add sound I mean," Allan mused aloud.

"That's worth a thought." His client took his fingers out. "Now scream for me, girl," he said, right before pushing the head of his penis straight past my sphincter.

And scream I did. He stopped and waited for me to stop. I was breathing heavily and tried to relax. It fucking burned!

With one thrust, he went all the way in and when his balls slapped my clit, I screamed until I grew hoarse. This time the pain and pleasure mixed. My mind couldn't comprehend what was happening. Shockwaves of the pain induced orgasm, went through my body. I squeezed his cock with my ass. He grunted as he pulled out and pushed back in.

"Oh God, it's too much, I-I-." And still I came when he forcefully pushed the whole length of his cock in and his balls connected with my clit. My walls were slowly getting used to his girth, and the throbbing didn't stop.

"Man, that Spanish Fly thing works wonders. I'm going to have to buy some for my wife. The woman is having problems lately with menopause and feeling depressed because of it. This might help."

The guy kept talking all the time he was slamming into me. Grunting, he pulled out of my ass with a pop and entered my sopping cunt. I hummed in delight. He leaned forward and touched my nipples.

When he pinched them, the sounds coming out of me would definitely not be misplaced in a porno. I couldn't help being vocal, and I hoped Allan understood. The guy kept pounding me with such force that the wooden structure I was bound to creaked in protest.

"Hand me the cunt cock-sleeve cylinder, Allan. It's better since I don't have to use a condom." The jacket disappeared from my head, and he jerked off with one of the cylindrical objects from the table. After he came, he took the thing off his cock and pushed a button on it. The humming noise from before stopped.

"The suction is really good. And even though your subject is nice and tight, I have to say, I prefer the sleeves."

I closed my gaping mouth at the spectacle and frowned at the comment.

"That's great news, I'll get the paperwork mailed to you this week, and I'll add a little bottle of the Spanish Fly droplets for free," Allan said.

The client put himself together, before nodding in Allan's direction.

"Good doing business with you Allan, I'm sure my investment will get a nice return."

Stunned, I stared as both men strode to another door, while I was still bound.

Chapter Eleven

Allan came back over to me after closing the door. He crouched, our gazes connecting, and stroked the hair out of my face. I hummed in pleasure, closing my eyes a second.

"You can speak freely now. How are you feeling?" He kissed me on the forehead and stood.

As he cleaned off the excess of lube with a moist cloth, he also caressed my aching clit with the rougher texture.

"Good," I answered honestly, moaning from the sensations.

"Are you all right to stay like this for a little longer?" He touched the cuff on my wrist.

I nodded. Apparently, he wasn't cleaning me up to release me. I tried to beg him with my eyes to fuck me but wasn't sure if that would have the right effect since he'd frowned earlier when I'd begged. He massaged more lotion on my pussy, and I had to bite my lip to keep from crying out. Why wouldn't he finish me off?

"You did very well. Can you handle another client?"

My eyes widened. What the hell? More? The hesitation must've been clear in my eyes as he crouched and gently kissed me on the lips.

"It's up to you. Same rules as before. Yes or no?"

"Yes," I whispered.

My pussy was still throbbing and far from satisfied. If he wasn't going to do it, maybe the next client would fuck me until the sensations stopped, or until I fainted.

"Very good. Be careful with the talking. I'll let the first one slide. The next will earn you a spanking," he warned.

Just the thought of being spanked spasmed my pussy. It made me wonder if I was going to want to be quiet to please him or if I would make noise to get a spanking?

A knock on the door announced the next client. My eyes widened at the vision that kissed Allan on the cheek before checking me out.

"Oh, Allan, what a lovely surprise," the speaker had a deep but feminine voice.

She was dressed from neck to toes in black latex that squeaked with every movement. Her languid pace was as smooth and comfortable as if she wore this type of outfit all the time. Her corset cinched in her tiny waist, flaring her hips gently, and the thigh-high, six-inch black boots raised her butt as she strolled into the room with catlike grace. Her blond hair and pale skin formed a huge contrast with the outfit, and to top it off, she had her nails and lips done in a burgundy red. She was stunning.

Crawling behind her, on her hands and knees, a skinny woman appeared. She wore latex as well, but it was red and barely covered her body. Just a bra and panties. The woman in black had the smaller one on a leash attached to a collar around her neck. Her mocha-colored skin complimented her short brown hair, which was long enough to cover her eyes whenever she put her head down.

Ms. Latex sauntered closer with her sub crawling behind her and stopped next to me. I held my breath. The woman stroked my back with the tips of her nails, goosebumps erupted all over my body and tightened my nipples.

"Lick them," she ordered, and I frowned not knowing what she meant since she wasn't anywhere close to my mouth.

Then a tongue slid over my tight nipples. She'd been speaking to the submissive woman. I moaned as she lapped at the tip of my left nipple. When she crawled underneath the wooden structure to my right nipple, her hair tickled my breast. It was both torture and bliss. She licked my other nipple, and the sensation went straight to my clit.

"That's enough." The woman pulled the leash, and the submissive passed underneath me again.

She sauntered to the table where Allan twirled a second glass of wine. When she sat, I noticed another strange contraption on the table in front of the woman. The girl positioned herself on her heels, her knees separated, her back straight and her hands on her thighs with her palms pointing upwards.

"You trained her well," Allan observed.

"Thanks. It took some time, but she's turning out to be a good addition to our dungeon." She petted the girl as if she was a dog.

A dungeon? Now that sounded interesting.

"When can we expect to see you again?" she asked.

"It depends."

"On this one?" She pointed in my direction.

My gaze darted between the two of them. His slight nod made my heart soar. I wasn't just being paid, I was being considered for...what exactly? I didn't know, but I liked the idea of sitting on the floor next to Allan. Having him pet my hair affectionately.

"Can't wait to watch you play again. And maybe you can teach this one a thing or two." She winked at Allan, and a small smile appeared on his face when he glanced at the girl.

Jealousy shot through me, and I almost opened my mouth. When his gaze connected with mine, he raised an eyebrow, and I thought better of speaking aloud.

"Let's get this presentation on the way, shall we? You said you had a new toy to show me that might be of interest for the dungeon's store?"

Allan rose and turned his back to me. He reached across the table, and I figured he was picking up the toy on the table.

"Yes, I believe it will be a nice addition to the dungeon and your personal collection."

I carefully studied their expressions. Both their eyes widened, and the woman clapped her hands.

"Yes, this definitely would be a nice addition. I take it we can try it out on your subject?"

"Of course. Would you or your sub be doing the honors?" Allan asked.

"I believe Maya has earned the honor for today. And if she can get your girl to scream, she'll get a bonus once we get home."

Scream? From pleasure I hoped, as I was burning up from the building orgasm again. Without something inside, I couldn't come, but I tried to grind my pussy into the leather nonetheless.

"Get up, Maya. Let's fit this contraption on you." The woman stayed seated while Allan commanded the girl. He handed Maya an odd-looking thing. She examined it for a moment before lifting one leg and stepping into it. From my point of view, I couldn't see what it was except for leather straps being attached to her hips. She turned and something protruded that I thought might be dildos and a flat piece that went between her legs.

"As you can see there are different options for sizes and wears. You can adjust it like this." He gave a pull on the links on the sides, almost lifting the girl off the floor.

She grimaced, but she didn't say a thing. The leather bit into the skin around her waist. After a few adjustments, Allan handed a remote controller to the woman.

"The way she's wearing it now gives her pleasure and allows for penetration while in this position. When the receiver is on her back, the pleasure pad can touch both of them."

Allan sat and crossed his legs. He held out a tube, which the girl took. She squirted some of it on the dildos and handed it back. She stalked towards me, and her submissive facial features changed to a devious expression that made me squirm. I still wondered about the screaming comment when it occurred to me that two dildoes meant double penetration.

"Before she starts, I have one request," Allan addressed the woman.

Maya froze next to me.

"Which is?" her Domme asked.

"Every time your sub comes, she needs to make the subject come."

"Agreed," she said with a smile.

She pushed a button on the remote, and Maya frowned. The buzzing of the pad between her legs was there to stimulate her clit. It was vibrating. Now it was my turn to grin. Not deviously but happily. She was definitely gonna make me come.

Maya stepped into position behind me, and she caressed my sides with her cool slender fingers. At first, she held onto my waist but the dildoes slipped left and right, not even close to the mark. I peaked out of the corner of my eyes. Deep concentration twisted her delicate features.

After a sigh, that could both be frustration and bliss since she was still buzzing, she grabbed onto both dildos and tried to push them into my pussy and ass at the same time. They tickled both places, but she couldn't penetrate me for some reason. I glanced toward Allan and the blonde. They were frowning, clearly unhappy with the performance.

With a frustrated sigh, Ms. Latex stood up and moved behind us.

"You hold onto the top one, and I'll slide in the bottom one," she ordered.

At once, the pressure on my rosebud built. I had to bite my lip when it became overwhelming. Thank god the other client had opened me up because Maya didn't care about going slow and gentle. I squeezed my eyes shut. When the top of the dildo slid past my sphincter I blew out my breath in a sigh of relief.

Then something entered my pussy, and my breathing hitched. Maya's nails dug into my sides as the dildos were slowly but steadily pushed inside both my holes.

I was breathing and perspiring heavily. The penetration didn't stop, and I was sure I was going to rip. Then the buzzing started. Both of the dildos vibrated. A moan and shudder behind me announced the orgasm of the girl fucking me with two dildos. Somewhere inside my haze, I remembered the promise that if she were to come, so was I. I was still on the edge but not close and was filled with disappointment when the dildos disappeared.

Her hair tickled my butt, and a wet tongue connected with my clit.

God, yes! This was more like it. Moaning and writhing I pushed my cunt into the tongue as well as I could.

"Lick it good, you little slut, you didn't ask to cum, so now I'll have to punish you."

I glanced behind me, and the woman towering over the kneeling girl situated between my legs, put her hand on the back of the girl's head and pushed her into my cunt. Her nose entered me, and she sucked my clit hard.

I came on a scream, creaming all over her nose.

"At least you made her scream," she mumbled.

Grabbing the sub by her hair, she stalked back to the chair. The girl stepped out of the contraption with a defeated look on her face, her head down.

"I believe your toy needs some work, Allan. I'll be expecting you next week in the dungeon with a new improved one and a proper punishment for my sub here. Are we in agreement?" Her voice was sharp as a whip.

"I'll let your tone of voice slip for now. But watch it, I don't mind binding and whipping you," Allan threatened in a deep voice. "I understand your frustration, and I'll check what I can organize by next week."

Walking to the door, he held it open. With her head held high, the haughty blonde walked out with her submissive girl crawling on her knees behind her.

Chapter Twelve

Allan leaned his head against the door for a moment. With a deep sigh, he pushed away and turned.

"Well, Greta, that concludes our meetings for today. A bit disappointing, but you did very well."

I beamed at him, proud of myself and loving his attention. It was a very odd feeling, but I liked it. When he stroked my hair, I hummed again, and he smiled.

Is he finally going to fuck me again? God, I hope so.

Even though I'd had quite a few orgasms already, I was still buzzing. The cream wasn't letting my body come down, keeping my senses at peak awareness and sensitivity.

"Now, before I release you, I have to confess something."

He crouched next to me and let his right hand slide over my back and down my left leg before moving up again on the inside of that leg. His hand reached my folds that were still open and wet from the girls' licking and my juices. He tapped my clit while he spoke, making it very hard for me to focus. Each tap was bringing me closer to orgasm.

"I put a few droplets of Spanish Fly liquid in your bottled water to make you hypersensitive and also covered your clit and nipples with something similar." He chuckled, "I just realized that I forgot to tell Madam Vera about that. Her subs' tongue is going to tingle for the rest of the night."

He shrugged. and his finger slipped inside my wet pussy. I kept quiet, wanting to moan, but also to please. He told me to stay quiet, and I'd already screamed. I needed more. And somehow I knew only he would do.

"Please," I whispered before I could stop myself.

A hard smack on my ass made me gasp.

"Wha-."

Another smack. I gazed up at him, and he had one eyebrow raised.

"Sorry, Sir," I whispered.

Tears were gathering. I'd disappointed him again, damn. He rubbed his palm over my bottom.

"It's okay, pet. You're new to this."

He started removing the shackles and cuffs from my wrists. Would the rest of my punishment be about not getting fucked by him? That would be cruel.

He rubbed my wrist and then put my hands behind my back.

"Hold your hands there," he commanded and stood up, "I'm going to fuck you now."

His zipper lowered, and he entered slowly. I purred like a kitten. He fit perfectly. Grabbing onto my hair, he lifted my upper body from the bench as far as it would go. I was stuck to the leather from sweat and winced as I came unglued. He took on a fast but steady rhythm rocking me on the wooden structure. My clit came hard into contact with the leather padding when he slammed forward and stayed there. I came undone with a low moan, which became a squeal when he pinched my right nipple. The pain made me contract hard on his cock, and he grunted while he thrust inside me, with short uncontrolled movements.

"Oh, yes," he moaned, as he came. The pulsing of his cock decreased and with it, his hard-on.

Withdrawing from me, he closed his trousers and released my ankles. Before I could hit the floor, he caught me in his arms. Lifting me bridal style, he walked over to the dungeon-like room where he put me on the love-seat.

"Are you all right to dress on your own?" he asked, making sure I made eye-contact when answering by putting a finger under my chin.

"Yes, Sir," I answered automatically.

"Good, take it nice and slow. Here's a fresh bottle of water, and I'll bring you home when you're ready." He handed me the bottle and kissed the top of my head.

"What about dinner?" I pouted.

"I think it would be better if you had a shower, some alone time to process all that's happened so far, and a good night's sleep. I have something I want to show you about tomorrow."

He tapped my bottom lip.

"Yes, Sir," I said, drawing out the words making my disappointment clear.

I stood, and he slapped my bottom.

"Good girl!" He smirked when I narrowed my eyes at him, upset over being sent home, and walked out the door that led into his office.

I could wait until tomorrow, surely. Patience is a virtue. I would keep myself busy tonight. Washing and cleaning my apartment weren't my favorite activity but needed to be done. That would take my mind off this whole new situation.

"Ah, there you are." He smiled at me with an almost fond gaze. "Are you ready to go?"

I nodded as he stood up from his desk and grabbed his coat. He led me downstairs where we were escorted into his limousine. I hadn't been expecting that. I'd expected him to drive me home like a normal person. Then again, I shouldn't have been surprised, considering the elaborate hidden rooms I'd just been in. Anyone who could create that in an office building, must be obscenely wealthy.

"I was wondering if you would be interested in being trained as my sub?" he said as we rode along.

"Really, Sir?" Hope fluttered in my chest.

"I noticed how you watched Maya and how eager you've been to do everything I've asked," he said. "It would mean a different contract, more suited to a submissive/dominant relationship."

"Um, okay," I stammered, my heart racing.

"We won't talk about it tonight. You need rest and food." He grinned at me. "I've taken the liberty of having my driver pick up Thai food for you. I know how much you love it."

"Oh yes, thank you." My mouth already salivated at the thought. Although, I had no idea how he knew what I liked.

"Tomorrow will give your body a chance to recover. I'll take you to dinner to discuss what being my sub would entail before you agree to anything." He wasn't requesting, merely stating a fact.

I nodded, wondering how I would be able to get through tomorrow pretending like I hadn't fucked the boss and a couple of clients, all in one day.

"If you have any questions, write them down, and then we will discuss it over dinner." He leaned forward and tapped my nose.

"Okay." I smiled.

It was going to be a long twenty-four hours.

Chapter Thirteen

By the time Allan dropped me off at my small apartment complex, I was a nervous wreck. The drive to my house had been filled only by me giving instructions on where to go, nothing else.

Opening the door, he handed me the bag with food, and waited by the limo until I'd gone into the building. I walked up the stairs, my legs shaking. I was tired not just from the client service, but from all the exposure I'd had to this new lifestyle. I'd been taken anally twice for the second time in my entire life. I orgasmed more in the past six hours than the last six months of my previous relationship. Double penetration was a definite new one, as was a woman licking my pussy.

Locking my apartment door behind me, I put the food on the small kitchen table, and turned on the TV for background noise, before undressing and taking a shower. My nipples were still sensitive, and staying under the stream too long hurt.

Wrapping my hair into a towel and drying myself, I was careful to avoid my breasts and clit. I pulled on my fluffy robe and slipped into my bunny slippers. Checking my face in the mirror, I didn't see anything different, even though I had a life changing experience. Maybe my eyes were a bit less innocent? I laughed at the stupid idea.

The whole time, his words kept playing through my head. Did I want to be his sub? Definitely. Did I know what that entailed? Not a clue. Today had been my first experience, and I'd enjoyed it, but guessed that this wasn't what it would be like in a dungeon.

It thrilled me when his eyes lit up when I called him Sir or when he smiled at me after I'd been a good girl.

A ding from my phone announced a text.

'How are you feeling?' It was from Allan.

'I'm good, thanks, how are you feeling?' I hit send before thinking about it.

I slapped my forehead. You idiot, what kind of reply was that?

Going over to the table to retrieve my food, I noticed inside the bag an envelope with my name handwritten on it. With trembling hands, I opened it.

Dear Greta,

I hope you enjoyed today as much as I did. As I've expressed my intentions to move forward with you as my possible submissive, I'd like to take you to a 'play' afternoon in a Dungeon. Not Madam Vera's but one from a close friend of mine.

You would be able to form your own opinion of what excites you and what not. We would be able to discuss everything during dinner afterwards.

There are a few rules you need to be aware of. You are not collared yet, but I'd like to protect you and as such it would be best if you stay by my side at all times.

Never talk to or approach people when they are 'playing'. Which is similar to what we did today.

We need to trust each other before any of this goes further, but to give you a taste, I'd like you to call me Sir and turn to me for permission to speak when spoken to. This is partly for us, but will show others that you are with me even though you aren't wearing my collar.

Let me know what you think. If you agree I'll have a package delivered to you tomorrow morning. Something to wear that is more appropriate than your office skirt.

Allan

Another ding announced a text message answer to my idiotic first reply.

'Happy to have had this experience with you. I hope you are looking forward to tomorrow.'

Looking forward to it? I was near screaming with excitement, hopping up and down in my bunny slippers, holding the letter close to me in one hand and my phone in the other.

Calming down, I thought carefully about my reply.

'Can't wait, Sir.'

I hit send with butterflies in my stomach. Finally, I sat at the table and dug into the box of Thai heaven with my chopsticks.

'For precautionary reasons, I'd like for you to give a friend the address for tomorrow. This is it...'

I swallowed and frowned at my phone.

'Why would I want to do that?' I texted back.

'In this world you are entering, safety and trust are two things. The first needs to always be there and you need to take care of some yourself. The second one needs to be earned. So for your own wellbeing I'm educating you on the basics. Let a friend know where you are, when going out for the first time with someone. Same as dating...'

The text was condescending. I blushed at my own ignorance, but he was right. I had to admire that he took the time to educate me on these basic things of not only BDSM but life in general. I was in my early thirties but apparently innocent in certain dangers of life.

'Okay, Sir.'

'Good girl.' Was the reply I got sent immediately after my text. It made me grin like an idiot. I loved being called a good girl by him.

I finished my dinner, cleaned up, and dressed in a red nighty. Tomorrow was Saturday, so I refused to set an alarm clock. I would hear the buzzer when someone arrived with my 'package'.

Even being excited, I fell asleep almost immediately.

Chapter Fourteen

Knocking woke me.

"I'm coming! Hold your horses," I shouted when they persisted.

Yanking the sash tight around my bathrobe, I hurried, barefoot, to my door, wincing at the cold floor.

"Yes?"

Opening the door a crack, I peered out, only to see an empty hallway.

I opened the door wider, clutching the bathrobe around my neck to keep the cold out. Sticking my head outside, I glanced left and right but didn't see anyone. Just as I was about to close the door, I noticed a package on the floor and everything that had happened yesterday, came back to me.

I picked up the box, hugged it close to my chest and hurried inside.

Putting it on the sofa, I stared at it.

"I'm going to need coffee to wake up first," I mumbled and darted to the kitchen to start the machine. While it dripped delicious black goodness, I chewed my thumbnail, still staring at the package. It was a plain cardboard box with my name and address stuck on.

Turning towards the machine, I sighed in relief that the coffee was ready. I nearly scalded my tongue on my first sip but the hot liquid slid down my throat and did wonders waking and warming me up.

I sat on the sofa with my legs folded under me sipping and sniffing my wake-up call, studiously ignoring the box.

It wasn't apprehension keeping me from opening it, I wasn't scared of what would be inside. I was excited and wanted to draw it out. So many options went through my mind of what kind of outfit Sir had sent me.

I put my empty mug on the table and pulled the box closer. Upon closer inspection, I would need a knife to open it. I ran to the kitchen, grabbed a knife, and sliced through the tape. The box's flaps popped open. Satin pink paper hid what was inside. Gently, I brushed it aside and gasped. I put my hand over my mouth to muffle the girlish scream trying to escape.

An honest to God corseted dress in red and black. Not only were they my favorite colors, but I'd always wanted to wear a corset. They were just so damn expensive.

In awe, I ran a trembling finger along the velvet and silk corset. The silk was black and the velvet red. A complicated pattern of fleur de lises decorated the top. Attached to the corset was a tulle black skirt. It was very short. I found something else underneath. Thigh highs and black heels. I was in seventh heaven and wanted Sir to know.

'Thank you so much, Sir! It's amazing.'

'You're welcome. I hoped you liked it. I'll pick you up around two PM. Make sure you have something to eat before we go. And afterwards, we'll have dinner.'

Next up was figuring out what to tell Natasha about this afternoon. Sir asked to send a message to someone to make sure they knew where I was. But I wasn't going to tell my friend that I was going to go to a BDSM club or dungeon.

No way, she was too prudish for that stuff. And I wanted to keep it a secret from my other friends for now.

In the end, I sent her a text that I was going on a blind date and would let her know if everything was or wasn't okay around four PM.

By two PM, I was dressed and already sweating. Getting that corset on alone wasn't easy. I nearly dislocated my shoulder trying to tie the bloody thing.

I let my hair fall loose and put mascara and lipstick on as makeup. The lipstick was miraculously the same red as the corset.

Putting a yellow raincoat over the whole ensemble seemed strange, but I didn't need my neighbours, or anybody else for that fact, seeing me in this ensemble.

I clung onto the railing with a death grip as these shoes weren't made to take the stairs like a lady.

I closed the front door of the building behind me and searched for Sir. Dominating the curb was a sleek, black limousine with a chauffeur stepping out. Slightly annoyed, I stood on my tiptoes hoping that Allan didn't think I was late if he was waiting somewhere else.

"Ms. Greta?" the driver of the limo asked.

I squeaked. "Uhm, yes?"

"I'm to escort you to the party," he stated straight-faced after which he opened the back door of the limo. I took a hesitant step forward and released a sigh of relief when I noticed Allan sitting in the back. Again a limo.

After I slid in, I undid the raincoat and revealed the outfit.

"Come here, Greta," he told me. I'd taken a seat across from him, so I maneuvered to the empty seat next to him.

"No, on your knees between my legs, sweet cheeks."

"Oh, of course, yes, Sir." I quickly did as he asked.

He grabbed my chin and raised my face to his. "You remember the rules?"

I nodded.

"If you want to try something extra this afternoon, you can discuss it with me in a whispered tone. And you stay by my side at all times unless I order you otherwise, understood?"

I nodded again.

"Questions are always answered by yes-Sir or no-Sir."

"Yes, Sir," I answered his question, lest I annoy him. I really wanted him to use me for both our pleasure and was well aware that this was a test for me to see if this world was something I'd enjoy exploring further and to prove to him that I could obey simple rules.

"Now, I do have a problem with you being dressed so hot…" He raised an eyebrow, and I got his drift.

With a grin I opened his leather belt and his black suit trousers. With the flat of my hand I rubbed him through his black shorts. While I did this, I was surprised to find an opening slit in them. Happy to have discovered this, I pulled his hard cock through the opening in his underpants.

When I licked my lips, admiring his member, he groaned. He watched me through half-lidded eyes. I kept eye contact when I licked him from the base to the tip. The little drop of pre-cum was salty on my taste-buds. I moistened my lips again and took the head in my mouth.

"Stroke my balls and take me as deep as you can," he commanded in his typical deep, dominant tone. With my left hand on his thigh, I reached under him and gently took his balls out through the opening. I went down inch by inch until his cock hit the back of my throat. I gagged a bit and pulled up.

I swirled my tongue around the head of his cock and dived, taking him deep into my mouth. With every downward move, he groaned.

"Now keep down as long as you can," he said softly, "and then keep your tongue moving."

I did as he instructed and tried to maneuver my tongue. I could only flick it to the left and right. I struggled to breathe, and my lungs began to burn.

I sucked my way to the head, swirling my tongue around the tip and slid it under the ridge. My breathing was ragged as I gasped for air.

"Again," he commanded. Just the order made my core contract, seeking for something. I squeezed my thighs together while I went down again.

I repeated the motion three times when he took a hold of my head and set the pace. Bobbing my head with both his hands, I clasped his thighs. I gagged here and there, but he didn't move too deep and quite fast, so breathing through my nose, I got it done.

When he pushed hard on the back of my head, I swallowed hard and his cock slid down my throat, gagging me. I tried to breath and swallow while he stroked my head, keeping it firmly in place. Then, with one tiny movement of my throat, he grunted as the jets of his cum spurted, almost choking me. I clenched and unclenched on his thighs, not wanting to dig my nails in them. I gazed up at him, tears streaming down my face. Staring into each other's eyes, he gently lifted my head off his cock. I was gasping for air when I finally came up. He stroked my tears away from my cheeks with his thumbs.

"Beautiful," he murmured.

If I hadn't been on my knees, I would have slid to the ground in a puddle. I wiped my mouth and raised my head, asking with my eyes for permission to get up.

"We have arrived."

Chapter Fifteen

The driver opened the door, and with a deep blush, I scrambled out of the car after Sir. When I straightened, I gazed at the mansion and gasped.

The place was two stories high and surrounded by greenery. The cobblestone road circled a fountain. The road extended past the fountain to allow for parking. A car idled, waiting for its passengers to climb out.

"Greta," Sir gritted between his teeth, getting my attention. "Close your mouth, girl."

My mouth snapped shut, and I dropped my gaze to my shoes. My last sighting was of a man smirking at the top of the stone staircase leading to the front door.His black hair was slicked back, and the strong nose combined with sharp cheekbones, reminded me of Sir.

"Brother, what a delightful surprise to see you here," the man yelled.

When we climbed the stairs, he hugged Sir and slapped him on the back.

Sir groaned."Greg, I live here."

My head snapped up, but I managed to keep my gaping to a minimum.He lives here? This was his house? What?!

"Greta, close your mouth, and say hello to my brother, Greg, who thinks he lives here."

I opened and closed my mouth before uttering: "How do you do?"

"Is this lovely creature your new sub?" Greg asked, surprise clear in his voice.

"That's what we're hoping to see today. We'll be observing, not playing."

"She'll be observing the scene, and you'll be studying her. Can't wait to see if you fit in our world." Greg winked at me.

I stood there as a mute, not sure what to make of him or the situation. Was I supposed to say something or nothing?

I searched Sir's gaze, and he just smiled. I smiled and ducked my head.

As we went inside, I saw all the splendour. He was filthy rich, and I hadn't even known. Why did he still have a job if he had a limo and a house half the size of the white house? He was the boss, but I didn't realize he owned the company. The entrance was all white, with a giant staircase that went up to the opposite wall to split in two. There were several doors on either side of the entrance. Out of one door came a maid who asked if she could take Sir's coat.

When she left, Greg and Sir conversed about the business and other things. Their voices droned in the background while I admired the paintings and the large vases with lillies. We passed the staircase to the back of the house. Another gentleman dressed like a fancy waiter opened an old wooden door leading under the house. He nodded at the two men, but didn't acknowledge me.

There was a soft melody coming from below as we descended. The stairs were worn from use. Careful not to slip with my heels, I held onto the railing.

When Greg opened the red velvet curtains, the music grew into recognisable beats. I caught my first glimpse of the hidden room.

It was breathtaking. A true dungeon, but with the luxury of black sofas and a stone bar off to the side. In the middle of the room was a girl dangling from the ceiling. Ropes bound her in what looked like a very uncomfortable position. Her arms were above her head, and she was almost bent double with her legs in front of her. Her breasts looked red, as if someone had bound them as well. A leather mask covered her eyes. That was the only piece of clothing she wore.

The right wall had a wooden cross with a guy bound to it. A metal contraption captured his cock, and a woman was attaching nipple clamps. His groans weren't muffled, but other grunts and even screams emanated from behind a curtain on the other side of the room. Something just as kinky must be going on back there.

"Would you like something to drink?" Greg was already at the bar and Sir waited, letting me take the time to see everything.

It was already all a haze, and I wasn't sure if alcohol was the right way to go. "Just water, please, Sir," I said.

Sir asked for a scotch and took both drinks to the row of sofas in front of the girl, swaying from the ceiling. I sat next to Sir with my back straight and my hands in my lap, observing.

Greg approached the dangling girl with a cane. He tapped her exposed thighs.

The next tap was harder, and it landed with a thud. The girl said nothing. Dangling from her hands and feet bent double, I imagined it must be hard to breathe. The next time he hit her, it was hard enough to elicit a gasp from her. A thin line turned bright red.

He hit her again a little higher, and the cane bit into the skin. This time, she groaned. He kept going, forming a pattern on her thighs. Here and there, he stopped to stroke the stripes left behind by the cane. As if he was admiring his work. He also paused to whisper to her.

"He's asking her if she is okay to go on," Sir informed me.

I jumped when the next strike landed and the girl threw her head back and wailed. Greg only waited like five seconds before striking again. She wailed again. Greg was paying more attention to her face than the welts he left on her skin. Another strike crossed the previous one and this time she shrieked. He dropped the cane on the ground and undid his belt.

Was he going to belt her next?

Nope. He undid his trousers and slid right into her pussy with a loud squelching sound that showed how wet she was. He slammed in and out of her, swinging her body by the ropes. Her head hung back, and her mouth was wide open, while her eyes were still covered.

"Now!" Greg commanded, and she started shaking uncontrollably, jerking the ropes. She was moaning loudly, and he grunted, "Good girl." After which she had another orgasm.

I grew wet and squeezed my legs together.

Greg had come as well and pulled up his trousers before releasing the girl from the ropes. She fell boneless against him, and he cradled her. He carried her to the sofa across from ours. I'm sure after all that time hanging her arms were numb. With a smile, he grabbed a blanket to cover what was obviously an exhausted but satisfied sub.

Chapter Sixteen

Taking a quick gulp of water, I stared with envy at the doting Greg and what he was doing to his sub. He was stroking her hair and murmuring things that made her blush and sigh in contentment.

"That's called aftercare. Both Dom and sub spend a lot of energy and emotion in a scene. Afterwards they both need each other for comfort and relaxation," Sir's hot breath caressed my neck while he spoke, keeping his voice low.

"This is what you are looking for from me?" I asked him in a whispered tone.

"This type of connection and contentment is what I reach for. For that to happen, the entire scene needs to pleasure both parties equally. Hence, me bringing you here to see what holds your interest." He draped an arm over the back of the sofa behind me.

"What did you like about the scene?" Sir asked me.

I bit my lip as I thought about it.

"I think I'd like the light tapping, not sure about the harder part and I loved the fact of being tied up and being helpless."

"And?"

"And I liked the interaction between them and satisfying the Dom." I nodded to myself.

"Good. For the next scene, I want you to try something," he said without glancing at me. He took his arm from behind me to reach forward to grab his glass of Scotch from the table that was between us and Greg. He took a sip and put it back down.

I set my water glass on the table next to his and put my hands in my lap.

He put his index finger under my chin to command my undivided attention. I stared into his eyes and was momentarily lost in them.

"I want you to remove your panties right here, right now and watch the next play sitting on my lap with your legs open." His gaze was so intense it took my breath away.

I nodded, which made him raise an eyebrow.

"Do I have to take you over my lap and redden that ass of yours?" He growled.

"Sorry Sir, Yes Sir," I stumbled over my words and quickly stood to remove my panties.

I focused only on Sir, as I didn't want to know who else was watching. The man at the cross, maybe? With his chastity belt on to prevent a full erection? Greg and his sub?

I didn't care. Actually, I cared. I wanted everyone to look and see that I was pleasing Sir. These feelings were confusing, and I tried turning my mind off.

I gave him my black panties, which he tucked away in his trousers pocket.

He patted his thigh, and I sat down gingerly, trying my best to put the very short teal skirt under my butt.

While I did that, there was some commotion in front of us, and I stopped fidgeting to take a peek.

A voluptuous red-head was being led towards the middle of the room. Her wrists had leather cuffs with metal rings, which the fully dressed man leading her, attached to the ceiling hook with rope. She wore a black leather eye-mask, similar to the previous girl, that covered her eyes, a ball-gag in her mouth and nothing else. The rope stretched her arms until her toes barely touched the wooden floor.

I jumped up slightly when I felt Sir's hand on the bare part of my thighs.

"Spread your legs as wide as you can and keep them open." I did as I was told.

"Now watch and tell me softly yes, Sir, when you see something you'd like to try. If you're getting close to orgasm, you must ask me if you can come."

His deep voice washed over me with that last command. I closed my eyes shortly, holding back a moan. How a man's voice could completely take control of my body and mind without even touching me was astonishing. But I craved that voice, I wanted it and I would do anything just to hear him call me a good girl.

"Yes, Sir," I whispered, already wet and breathless.

His cock pressed into the small of my back, and I had to resist wiggling against him. Keeping my legs open was harder than it should have been. Whenever he moved in his seat, I moved along. His legs were slightly open between my thighs. It was only the high heels and four-inch plateau's under my shoes that made it possible for me to keep my feet on the ground.

The cool air caressing my pussy caused my inner muscles to clench on the emptiness waiting to be filled.

I was so focused on Sir's hard cock behind me that the sharp sound of leather on bare skin made me flinch. Jerking my gaze up, I focused on the scene in front of me. The fully dressed man was using a leather flogger on the woman's naked butt. She swayed on the tips of her toes upon impact. It was both erotic and hot. He went about the flogging methodically. Hitting harder with each swing.

I wiggled on Sir's lap, finding it hard to keep still as I watched.

"Did something catch your eye?" His hot breath caressed my ear.

"Yes, Sir," I answered.

"Good."

Just as Greg had, the man approached his sub to whisper in her ear. She nodded.

He grabbed another implement from the bag near him. A horsewhip. Even the lighter tap made a loud smacking sound. I could see her buttocks moving with each hit. They were growing bright red.

"Yes," I whispered.

I felt my face flush and my nipples tightened. I was breathing so hard that my breasts were coming over the corset.

Chapter Seventeen

"Very good."

Sir's hands were now on my knees and slowly moved towards my cunt. He avoided touching it, instead moved higher up my body. He reached into my corset from the top and grabbed my breasts. Lifting them out of the cups gave me some much needed room to breathe. When he pinched my nipples in combination with the woman getting her nipples hit by the horsewhip, I nearly came undone. The woman screaming was an extra aphrodisiac, I was ashamed to admit to myself.

"Yes?" he asked.

"Oh, yes," I sighed.

The man caressed the woman with the horsewhip, moving lower over her abdomen, tapping her thighs.

"Open," I heard him order.

The woman tried her best, since she was already on tiptoes. The space she created was just enough for the whip to hit her right on her open cunt, causing her to moan loudly.

I moaned as well and was rewarded by an open-handed slap on my pussy. I screamed together with the redhead as she got a second hit on her pussy. We came together. I collapsed against Sir without taking my eyes from the scene.

The woman slumped into the cuffs, her entire body weight held by her wrists. The man dropped the horsewhip and put one arm around her torso so he could lift her up enough to loosen the knot. She dropped, sobbing, as he held her close.

"Sometimes the emotions in a scene can be overwhelming," Sir told me.

"Now, as for you...You didn't ask permission to come," he pushed me up to a standing position, "I believe a proper spanking is in order, don't you think Greta?"

I didn't know what to say. I wanted to try everything, but was I a pain slut or was I going to scream bloody murder at the first hit?

I didn't want to embarrass myself, let alone him.

"Lie down on my lap, ass in the air and remember your safe word: Pear."

The commanding tone of his voice made me wet, and I knew there and then I'd do anything this man asked in this lifestyle.

I happily complied, arranging my body over his legs. He shifted me around, and I ended up nearly keeling over onto the ground head first. I quickly put my hands down to keep from falling. He swept my skirt aside. Closing my eyes, I enjoyed the feeling of his large hand exploring my backside while his other hand held the back of my neck firm, keeping me in position.

The first hit elicited a yelp. It wasn't hard, but I was caught by surprise. He stroked the left cheek where he'd spanked and followed it with a quick spank on the right one. Again I yelped. Even though I didn't struggle to come up, I felt his grip on the back of my neck tighten and boy didn't that make me wet. Against my side, I felt the bulge of his cock growing. Again, he soothed the spot he'd hit.

The next hit didn't surprise me with the timing, but with the force. He wasn't going soft on me now. He was building up the strength of his slaps and methodically moved from one cheek to the other. I was squealing and moaning and kicking my legs. When he stopped to caress, I felt heat coming off my ass cheeks from the blows. I stopped struggling and moaned in delight. The heat from my ass was spreading to my pussy, and when the pain subsided, I wanted more.

As if he knew, he started over, until I was on the verge of calling my safe word. Right before I would, he stopped. Tears were streaming down my cheeks, but I felt pride blossom inside me at the simple fact that I hadn't used my safe word. It was the strangest thing. Pussy juices pooled inside me and dripped down my legs. Both of his hands were caressing my ass now, moving lower and lower to my pussy. I couldn't hold back the whimpers and moans. I bit my lip to keep myself from begging. I wanted his fingers inside me on my clit, anywhere to make me come. I was desperate, but knew instinctively that if I begged, he would stop.

Ever so slowly, he descended from the slopes of my buttocks to the crease underneath. I wiggled my butt and opened my legs a bit, which elicited a chuckle.

"You've made me so hard from being such a good girl. You took more than I thought you could handle. And I can read your body and cries easily. But now I want to give you a reward. Do you want to come by my fingers or cock?"

I had to hold myself back from coming just by hearing those words in his husky, deep voice.

"By cock, please, Sir," I whispered.

He put me upright. I swayed but could focus enough to see him opening his trousers right in front of me.

"Climb on, pet and we can both enjoy this ride." He patted his lap.

He didn't have to tell me twice. I put one knee on the side of his legs and lifted myself over his cock, putting my other knee on the other side. Our gazes locked and his pupils had widened.

"Now," he ordered, and I sank down in one swift move. Both because I couldn't wait anymore and I couldn't keep my weight on my knees for much longer.

"Yes, such a good girl," he grunted out, and I dropped my head on his shoulder, savouring the words and the feeling of him deep inside, stretching me to my limits.

I lifted, and we both moaned. Throwing my head back, I gave him the advantage of sucking my nipples. The pulling of his lips, shot straight to my clit. I was just in time to ask: "Can I come, Sir?" but before he could answer, I was already there, spasming around him.

He lifted me off of him and stood. He twisted me and pushed me down so I had to bend over and put my hands flat on the sofa. Without waiting, he plunged his cock into my wet pussy and pounded into me at a fast pace, grabbing onto my still sore ass. Another orgasm shot through my body, taking my breath away. He fell forward as he went over the edge as well. Breathing heavily, he extracted himself and took a napkin from his pockets to clean both himself and me. I was still bent over when he sat down next to me and took me in his arms to cuddle me as Greg had cuddled his sub.

Utter bliss.

Chapter Eighteen

After that spanking introduction and the most intense orgasm I'd ever had, I couldn't stop smiling. Somehow, Sir had known when to slow down, when to hit harder, and when to stop.

The experience had been divine, but now I was starving. Sir decided we could leave the Dungeon and have a bite to eat. This meant me sitting down on a chair. I wasn't too happy about it and grimaced while trying to sit in a way that didn't hurt. I met his smug smile with a sneer. He raised an eyebrow, and I turned my head.

We were in the dining room of his house. I should say mansion. I mean, it totally was. The dining room was more like a ballroom, and I was pretty sure my entire apartment could fit inside. A large painting of a gory hunting scene over the fireplace stared down at us. I tried to ignore it.

I sat at one end of this enormous table and he on the other. Three empty chairs on each side separated us. In front of me was more silverware than I'd ever seen for one meal. Was I supposed to use something different for every bite? I took a nervous sip of water from the sparkling tumbler sitting in front of my plate.

A maid appeared with two plates full of delicious smelling food. She stopped beside his chair and waited for Sir to show he was ready to be served and set a plate in front of him. She then moved over to my side and served me. My mouth watered at the sight of the roast with veggies. I was so focused on the food that I hardly noticed the maid left until she returned a moment later with a pitcher of red wine. She filled the wine goblets in front of us and left.

"To an interesting afternoon," Sir said, lifting his glass.

I raised my glass and took a sip. The wine was rich and dry, just the way I liked it. I took a second sip and put my glass down. I grabbed the first fork and knife next to the dish, but the clearing of a throat interrupted me from attacking the food. Glancing up, I saw Sir watching me. Frowning, I waited for an explanation.

"For now, it's all right, but in the future, it's always presumed that the Dominant will take the first bite."

Interesting. Kind of like in the Middle-ages, servants last. At least I didn't have to wait until he finished. As if he'd read my mind, he continued.

"In some relationships it's agreed that the Dominant or Master eats his or her meal first, but I like the company, so that's one rule I have," he said followed by taking a bite of his roast, "Do you have any objections to that rule?" he asked after swallowing.

I shook my head. "No, Sir, no objections."

He nodded and continued eating. Our eyes connected once every so often and I couldn't stop watching him licking his lips. It made me hot all over again. I decided to see if I could turn the tables on him and slowed down. I lightly moaned and closed my eyes while chewing on a piece of juicy meat. Sipping the wine, I used my tongue to lap up a stray droplet.

"If you keep that up, you won't be getting any sweet dessert," Sir growled.

"I don't mind if it's salty, Sir," I answered with a cheeky grin.

He got up and rounded the table. Before I knew what was happening, he'd lifted me from the chair, grabbing me by the throat, and gave me a punishing kiss. My knees felt weak, and I moaned into his mouth as our tongues dueled. With a sharp nip to my bottom lip, he stopped the kiss and dragged me over to the side of the table.

Throwing a chair that was in his way to the ground, he lifted me up onto the surface. My breath caught with excitement. Pushing me back on the table, he positioned me the way he wanted. One hand was between my breasts, holding me down while he fumbled with his trousers. I hardly knew what was happening as he pulled his belt off and, in an expert move, bound my ankles together. Lifting them up, he leaned forward, putting his head through the space created. His pants dropped to the floor. One hand guided his cock and his other opened my pussy. He entered me slowly, and I pulsed around him the moment his head passed my g-spot.

He leaned forward, moving my legs with him. Grabbing onto my wrists, he held them next to my head to both restrain me and to keep his full weight off of me. Slowly, he thrust in and out. I tried to wriggle, but he had my limbs arranged in such a way that, except for moving my hips a bit, there was nowhere for me to go. He wasn't touching my clit, but I came undone anyway, purely from being restrained. He smirked as he gazed deep into my eyes, pulling out of my still throbbing body.

"Ready for your dessert?"

My eyes widened, and I nodded. "Yes, Sir."

He rotated my body on the smooth surface of the table so that my feet were on the opposite end and my head was falling off, right in front of his cock, now coated in my juices.

My mouth opened eagerly as he guided his cock forward. I wet my lips, which elicited a groan from him. Inching forward, he entered my mouth. I swirled my tongue around the bulbous head when he kept still. He pushed further and started up a rhythm of slow, shallow thrusts.

"Use your tongue a bit more," he instructed me huskily.

I complied and wiggled my tongue as much as I could. His girth was making my jaw hurt and left little room for my tongue to move. Slowly, his shallow thrusts went deeper and deeper. I gagged once, twice and tried to focus on keeping my gag reflex under control. When his fingers painfully pinched my nipples, I gasped, and he moved in all the way to the back of my throat.

"Ah, yes, that's it," he murmured.

Tears were streaming down my face from the lack of oxygen, and I squirmed.

"Keep still," he ordered.

Once I did, he withdrew his cock until only the head was in my mouth. I breathed heavily through my nose, saliva dribbling from the corners of my mouth into my hair, mixing with the tears. All I wanted was to please him. When his upper body moved forward, I took a deep breath, preparing for him to enter again.

"Keep that tongue of yours busy."

The moment I did, he rewarded me with a finger moving between my pussy lips. He coated it with my juices and slid to my clit, slowly circling it. I gargled around his cock, needing his finger right on top of my clit, not around it.

As if he heard my thoughts, his finger zeroed in on my clit, touching it the way I needed. My hips moved, wanting more. All the while, I kept my tongue active on his cock.

I squealed when he pinched my clit and that gave him the opportunity to push his cock all the way down my throat again.

"God, that feels so good," he groaned.

He kept massaging and circling my clit, now with two fingers. When I struggled again, he withdrew. I barely caught my breath before he moved forward and pushed two fingers deep inside my wet cunt. I came instantly, and he took advantage of my orgasm to wrap his hands around my neck, pushing down with his thumbs. He didn't go slow now, his strokes were fast and deep. I tried to find a rhythm to take in some oxygen here and there.

"Hmmm, I can feel and see my cock moving in your throat."

He was breathing faster and hearing his voice deepening, I was proud of what I'd achieved. For the first time I'd managed to deep throat, something I'd never done before because of my gag reflex. Sir was treating my body as a finely tuned instrument.

Grunting, he pushed in deeper still and I felt his cock pulse against the inner walls of my throat and my lips. I swallowed everything. He removed his now softening penis and I could finally breathe. Gasping and sputtering, I turned to my side. He pulled up his trousers and helped me sit up on the table.

"Gods, Greta, you look beautiful with your tears." His gaze was soft.

He took my head in his hands and gently wiped away my tears, before smashing his lips on mine. I used his necktie to pull him closer and wrapped my legs around his waist.

With a sigh, he stopped the kiss and put his forehead against mine.

"I would really like to train you to be my sub," he whispered, his eyes closed.

"I'd like that very much, Sir," I answered in a whisper, not wanting to break the spell.

Chapter Nineteen

"I want you to work as my personal secretary from here for the next week. You'll need to stay here day and night. We'll train once every day unless something else comes up. We can try 24/7 the week after," he said.

I swallowed hard, trying to follow what he was saying. My mind was blown.

"What does that entail exactly?" I asked.

"Well, being my secretary would entail doing your regular work, during business hours, of course."

He helped me off the table, taking his belt from around my ankles. Grabbing my hand, he led me to the next room, which had the same style of sofa I'd seen at his apartment. The room was a replica, including a fireplace and designed in warm Bordeaux colors with wooden panels and flooring.

"Why do you have a house in the city and one here?" I wondered without really consciously directing the question to him.

"Because I keep my private life private. The office and city living arrangements are separate to make sure no one knows where I truly live."

"But why? ... Uh, Sir."

"I'm a very wealthy man, but as far as anyone knows, I'm a simple businessman who sells erotic toys on the side. I'd like to keep it that way, therefore I'm going to have to ask that you sign a confidentiality contract. You can also make a list of everything you want to try, and everything that's absolutely off limits for you."

"So, no one knows you live here?" I cocked my head.

"No, and my real name isn't Allan Devon either." He smiled. "But you will only know me as Sir." He winked.

I gaped at him and suddenly jumped up. I can't believe I'd forgotten Natasha!

"Everything alright?" he asked, frowning.

"Yes, but I forgot to call my friend, she's going to be worried sick!"

I ran to my purse in the dining room and rifled through it to find my phone. I had set it on vibrate, and there were several missed calls and a few messages.

Her phone only rang once before she picked up.

"Hi, Natasha!" I was out of breath.

"Are you alright? I called you like five times! I was about to call the police!"

"Calm down, I'm fine, just forgot to call you." I rolled my eyes at her exaggeration.

"Having that much fun, are you?" I heard her grin through the phone.

"Yes, yes, I am," I gloated. We were best friends since high school. We knew all of each others' dirty fantasies.

"Spill, girl! Wait, I've got some juicy news too! Remember that guy at work always checking me out but never really doing anything about it?" She didn't wait for an answer. "I saw him an hour ago going into that sauna club!" She squealed so loudly I had to hold the phone away from my ear.

"You're going there tonight?"

It always shocked me when she talked about going to 'the club'. It was a swinger's sauna. She never had the courage to go, and I hadn't been interested to be her wing woman. Now she was going alone, because some guy she fancies was going as well? It was dangerous. But sometimes Natasha was more adventurous than I.

She'd be proud of me if I told her about the last couple of days, not that I had a chance to say anything more.

"Yes, I'm going in now! Be safe, alright!"

"I will and the same goes for you!"

She hung up before I could finish my sentence

When I entered the sitting room again, Sir's frown was still on his face.

"Everything alright?" he asked.

"Yes Sir, Natasha is fine," I answered and felt my cheeks heat.

"What's with the blush, Kitten?" Sir asked.

My cheeks heated up even more. He'd called me by a pet name. That simple, one word endearment made me feel really special.

"It's because she went to a 'club' following a guy from work."

"A club?" Sir raised an eyebrow, "That's nothing to blush about…"

"It's a swingers sauna club… naked, Sir."

Standing there gazing at my fingers, I wondered why something like that made me blush when he had seen me fully naked multiple times.

"I know clubs like that. Some even do a BDSM themed evening. We might check one out one day if you want to."

Gaping like a fish, I looked up at him.

"I don't know, Sir, I-I-I." I stuttered.

"You don't have to decide right this instant, Kitten. Don't worry about it. For now, I believe it would be a good idea for you to retire to one of the guest bedrooms." He stood up from the sofa and finished his drink in one swallow.

"But I don't have any clothes with me, Sir," my protest sounded lame, but I hadn't really expected to spend the night.

"Greta, do you agree to be my submissive in training?"

"Yes, Sir, I do," I answered without hesitation.

"Then you have nothing to worry about. As long as you are in training and maybe after, I will look after you."

"Thank you, Sir!"

"Don't thank me yet. We have regular work to do tomorrow, and in the evening, your training will take place. Now let me show you to your room."

He held out his hand, and I put my much smaller one into it.

Chapter Twenty

"**T**his is the place where you are to report tomorrow morning."

Sir led me into a gigantic kitchen with a cooking island in the middle. Everything was white, grey and shiny, as if no one had been in there except to clean the place.

There was a round oak table off to the side with a view over the garden through large windows. The only color were the large curtains. They were again in Bordeaux red.

"You will take whatever position you choose at my side and wait for my order to eat, is that understood?"

Frowning, I shook my head. "Position, Sir?" I asked as he led me out of the kitchen.

"In your room is a small manual from which you can choose any position pictured in it. Each position is explained. You will need to learn all of them, but for now you can choose one. That one will need to be shown tomorrow morning, naked," he added the last word casually.

At that, I stopped walking.

"What about the maid?" I squeaked.

"She won't be present by the time you come downstairs. She makes breakfast and leaves it. She won't return until lunch to prepare dinner and do some cleaning. Now enough with the questions. We're here." He stopped.

We'd passed the staircase and were near the dungeon door. No one was there right now and all was quiet. I wondered where his brother had gone. Opening my mouth to ask, I shut it again when he opened the door to my 'room'. It was a suite fit for a queen. My eyes went wide as I took in the view. A huge four-poster bed dominated the room with three doors that led to god knows where.

"On the bed is the manual. Have fun and good night." Sir kissed my forehead and gave me a small push to enter the room so he could close the door.

Large ceiling to floor windows showed the sun setting over a beautifully manicured lawn. A set of glass doors opened to a terrace with a quaint metal table and chairs. I twirled around in the room and opened the first door I saw. My mouth nearly dropped to the floor. It revealed a walk-in closet with a floor length mirror on one end. Seriously, it was the size of a small dress shop! It looked like one too, fully stocked with dresses, suits, pencil skirts and blouses. Flashy dresses with shoes in every shade and height imaginable. All perfectly my size.

In the middle was a tall armoire. Curious, I opened the doors and pulled open the drawers, one at a time. Inside was lingerie that made me blush. Bras with cups and without cups. Panties with crotches and without. Jarretelles, fishnet stockings, bustiers. Some jewelry was there as well, but not the kind to put around your neck or in your ears. One that caught my eye was a butt-plug, sparkling in the midst of all that glorious lace and leather.

I took out a naughty, see through, red lace nighty that didn't leave much to the imagination. Only my breasts would be decently covered. It was more of a baby doll nighty than something to sleep in properly. Then again there wasn't anything there that looked like it was meant to sleep in. I chuckled, as I mostly slept nude anyway, so it wasn't a problem. It was just fun to try on the clothes that were far sexier than anything I'd ever owned before.

Opening the second door I found a simple toilet and bidet. I didn't need to use it, so I shut the door and moved on to door number three. I opened it and started giggling, which soon turned into a proper laugh. Clapping my hands, I went closer to inspect. It was a bathroom. A white bathtub, which on closer inspection I found was a jacuzzi which could easily fit two people, stood against a black tiled wall.

Shampoo bottles and bath salts were arranged on the side. When I turned to the sink I noticed a toothbrush and toothpaste still in its original package. There was also quite a large assortment of tiny bottles of soap and body lotion. One tube was clearly recognizable as the lotion I'd used to rub over my body before servicing the clients the other day. My grinning face was reflected in the large mirror above the sink.

I was dead tired, but was sure I could stay awake long enough to enjoy a hot bath. Checking the bath salts I searched for something to relax my aching muscles and soften the sting on my butt. There was one that had arnica in it and would do just the trick. Turning on the tab I checked for the right temperature and let it run.

While the tub filled, I ran over to the bed and picked up the manual which consisted of only four pages. Taking it back to the bathroom I read the first page and realized it was the rules for what would be expected from a collared sub after concluding the training.

Some were easy and already known to me; not talking unless talked to, answering with yes, Sir or no, Sir, waiting before starting a meal until he took his first bite, and not talking or looking at other Dom/mes unless talked to. Greeting Sir in the morning fully naked and awaiting instructions, while taking the 'bracelettes' position, was a new one.

Putting the manual down next to the bath I struggled to take off the corset. By the time I was finished I had to hurry to turn the taps off, as the tub was close to running over. I added the bath salts and stepped into the water with a deep sigh of contentment.

I closed my eyes for a minute and sank deeper, completely relaxed.

I'd left the manual next to the tub and reached for it to read the rest of the directions. It consisted of six positions with their respective purpose. The last page was six pictures of the positions that were posed by a very sexy naked woman. I felt my core clench just looking at these pictures. They weren't lewd but erotic. I had to flick back and forth between the description pages and the picture page to fully understand which meant what.

When everything became clear I was horny as hell and knew exactly which position I was supposed to take in the morning but also knew which one I was going to practice before bed. It was a different one. It called the pleasure slave position, in short Nadu. The sub was to face the Dom/me or Master, sink to his/her knees, lean back so the weight was supported by the heels with a straight back and knees opened as wide as possible. You needed to lift your head up and open your mouth. Hands were to rest on the legs, palms up.

Just thinking about it, I could imagine the pleased look on Sir's face. Maybe he would be disappointed I didn't choose the more conservative Bracelette's position as it was very similar, except for the knees being closed, arms crossed behind the back and eyes cast down.

It was still early, so I had time to practice both since after my soak in the tub I was totally revived.

Once I was dry and sitting on the bed, I glanced at the pictures again. Trying the pleasure position on the bed wasn't easy therefore I went over to the walk-in closet and sank to my knees in front of the mirror. Like this I could watch myself and check for errors in my posture in comparison to the sexy woman in the pictures.

My back started to ache after practicing for half an hour and on a yawn, I got up and went to bed. Once my head hit the pillow I fell asleep.

Chapter Twenty one

A phone call from Sir woke me up. I jumped out of bed, eager to see where this day would take me. As I was about to enter the kitchen I remembered I was supposed to be naked. I ran back and discarded the silky robe I'd slipped into.

Running into the kitchen, I took the pleasure position next to his seat. He smirked and patted my head before leaning down to grab my chin and kiss me.

I started to get up, but he stopped me with a sharp order.

"Bracelettes."

I gaped at him as my mind raced. Quickly I changed my current position to the one he requested, or rather demanded.

"For getting up before I told you to, you will get five strikes tonight. It would normally be ten, but because you quickly took the other position, I'm halfing it. Any indiscretion before or after work, which consists of eight am till four pm, will be punished as I see fit, is that understood?"

"Yes, Sir," I answered humbly.

If I wanted to show I was serious, I realized I'd better stay in position until he ordered me otherwise.

"Good."

The food smelled amazing, but he still hadn't told me I could get up when he took his first bite. My stomach churned in protest when it realized it wasn't getting food anytime soon. Damn, this was not going to be as easy as I'd thought. Probably why Sir had said I would need to train for a while.

He had started eating but still hadn't ordered me to get up to sit and eat as well. This confused me since he'd told me yesterday that he wouldn't do that. Was this another test?

"Released," he said.

I glanced up. He sipped his coffee while reading the paper. An actual newspaper on paper. How old fashioned. Getting up, I took one step in the direction of my room, when he stopped me.

"Where do you think you're going?" He raised an eyebrow.

"Getting dressed for breakfast and work." I clenched my fists, keeping my voice level. Should I have asked permission for that as well?

"You will eat first before getting dressed for work and I do believe you know by now that you always add 'Sir' to a sentence." He narrowed his eyes.

Crap, I'd forgotten already.

"Yes, Sir, I'm sorry, Sir," I mumbled, casting my eyes down.

"I guess we'll be adding five, which makes a total of ten. At least for now you can choose what I'll be using and where. You will lose these privileges if there are more transgressions in the next hour and the two hours before dinner."

I kept my mouth shut and moved toward the only other chair at the table. It wasn't as comfortable as the one Sir sat one. I was very aware that the wicker weave in the seat would be disagreeable to my bare bum. All I could think was that it was going to leave marks. There weren't any real bruises on my butt but it still smarted from the spanking last night and I carefully took my seat.

The sight of a scrumptious spread of bacon and eggs in the middle of the table made my mouth water. When I saw the chocolate breakfast buns, I forgot about the pain in my butt and indulged in a delicious breakfast.

When I'd finished, I remembered to ask Sir if I could be excused to get dressed. He smiled and nodded.

After getting dressed the usual boring secretary business took place. When I'd dressed I grabbed the panties and bra in the armoire that looked the most comfortable. They weren't. Every so often I had to run to the toilet so I could adjust the freaking lot. It kept moving up or down or in between my pussy lips. While I was pretty sure that was the point, I had to focus on work.

I joined him in his home office where the tiny desk and rigid wooden chair were in sheer contrast to his large mahogany desk and luxurious leather chair. He stood in front of me and handed me the dictaphone. Sir started rambling off notes, which I jotted down.

I plugged in the earphones to start typing the document. He left while I was busy. When he came back he grabbed the dictaphone and recorded the next document while I was still doing editorial work on the previous one. I was halfway through when it was time to head to the kitchen for lunch.

The salad looked like it came from a delicatesse store. The maid was already preparing dinner and it smelled delicious. I shyly attempted to smile at her but she never made eye contact. I went back to the office.

Another four hours of typing later and I cracked my fingers. Finally the second document was finished and I'd even been able to read it over and correct mistakes. I hit send and sighed in relief. I arched my back and shut down the computer.

"Greta, please present yourself in the bracelettes position in thirty minutes in the dungeon." Sir's voice spoke over the intercom. I pressed the button to answer.

"Yes, Sir."

He'd told me there was going to be two hours of training and searching for my limits with certain devices before dinner. I would have to keep up with the rules. Every transgression would lead to an increase of my punishment. I wasn't sure I could handle getting my breasts or anything but my ass being spanked. My bottom was all I was prepared to handle. If I wasn't careful, I wouldn't have a choice in the implements used or the place of my body he would use them on.

On one hand, I would love to give him that control, on the other, I struggled with it.

81

Chapter Twenty two

After a quick shower, I looking for something decent to temporarily cover my nudity and practiced the position. It took up so much time that I had to hurry to the wooden door that led to the dungeon at the time Sir had requested.

I carefully tiptoed down the stairs. This time it was eerily quiet.

I had no clue where to take the position. Glancing around, I draped the silk bathrobe that had barely covered me, over one of the lush sofas and walked tentatively to the 'stage' where the other women had been yesterday.

Sinking to my knees, I put my butt on my heels, my hands behind my back as high as I could. I frowned. What came next? Was it head up or down? Damn, I couldn't remember so I decided to go down as the pleasure slave position was up. Straightening my back, I could already feel the ache between my shoulderblades.

One minute turned into two minutes. My feet were falling asleep and I knew there would be pins and needles hell to stand up. I realized my everyday posture must be horrendous as I had to constantly readjust my position to straighten my back.

After five minutes I started to wonder if I'd read the clock on my nightstand wrong. Maybe I was early? I didn't dare change position as I knew this could well be a test. The first of many.

"Very good, Kitten," a deep voice commented from the shadows somewhere to my left.

At the last second I reminded myself to keep still. I'd almost blown it by turning my head in the direction of his voice.

"Close your eyes," he ordered, and without hesitation I did.

I felt his heat before he touched me, running the back of his hand along the side of my face. Slowly his hand lowered until he suddenly gripped my neck and kissed me deeply. I moaned in the back of my throat, my hands itching to touch his chest and pull him closer. My excitement had ignited and I really wanted him to take me right there. While he was kissing me I imagined him pulling me up, pushing me against the wall face first and thrusting his cock inside. Between my fantasy and the reality I was sopping wet. He ended the kiss but kept the hold on my neck. Tight enough for me to feel it but not to bruise.

"I'm going to blindfold you and then it's up to you if you want to be cuffed or not. Think your answer through. You won't be allowed to move without consequences." His voice rasped.

He moved behind me and slipped on the blindfold. Biting my lip, I was unsure if I wanted to let go of all control.

"You will not be gagged, your safe-word will always be in play." His baritone reverberated through my body, tightening my nipples and eliciting spasms from my empty pussy.

"Cuffed, please, Sir," I decided with a husky voice.

"Good. First, lean forward in the 'kneeling to the whip' position." I did as he bid me, bending forward until my tummy was resting on my knees. My forehead touched my crossed wrists and my sensitive nipples grazed the carpeted floor. I heard some rustling behind me and, not knowing what to expect, tensed. I felt a drop of something cold on my asshole. When his finger started circling around it, I tensed even more.

"Relax, I'm not going to hurt you...much," the chuckle in his voice annoyed me so much that I relaxed enough for his finger to enter.

The sensation made me gasp and I tensed again. Slapping my ass lightly, he ordered me to relax. I took a deep breath and was able to relax enough for him to move his finger around a bit.

"Swirl your tongue around this and make it wet enough for entering."

I'd had to turn my head sideways and did as told. A metal tasting oval instrument was pushed in my mouth. He used the same rhythm with his finger as with the metal thing, which I presumed was a plug. It wasn't very big but at the biggest part at least two fingers. The moment it crossed my mind, he pushed a second finger in my ass. When that didn't form a problem, he pulled the plug from my mouth. I felt another droplet of liquid which he rubbed around his still moving fingers.

In one swift move he replaced his fingers with the plug. The feeling was intense but not painful. I took deep breaths struggling to relax around the metal intruder. Once I was used to it, I breathed normally again.

When he tapped the bit still sticking out, I gasped. It didn't go any deeper, I just felt the tap and clenched around the plug involuntarily. It was an affirmation to let me know that even though I had relaxed, it was still there. He could make me tighten around it anytime he wanted to make sure I didn't forget who was boss. I heard some jingling next to my head.

"Hands forward," he ordered. I pushed up from my position on the ground to offer my hands, the plug moving around. Leather cuffs enveloped my wrists.

"Stand."

I struggled when the pins and needles started and the uncomfortable feeling of the butt plug. My mind was whirling, trying to decide which of the two it would concentrate on. When I lost my balance, he steadied me. He lifted me up and arranged my body onto a flat surface until he was satisfied. My butt was on the edge of what I thought was a wooden table. Bending my knees, he put some sort of restraint on my thighs and shins, making sure my knees remained bent with my feet on the table next to my butt. It was a position my body wasn't used to and my muscles strained to get comfortable. It kept my pussy wide open and the cool air tightened my clit. I felt him put cuffs on my ankles and link them to my wrist cuffs.

"Everything alright, my delicious slut?" he asked, running his hands up and down my body.

Goosebumps erupted everywhere. I felt a sharp pain in my left nipple.

"I asked you a question," he growled.

"Yes, Sir, sorry, Sir, everything is alright, Sir," he released my nipple at my rushed answer.

"I will be testing some clamps on your pussy lips and nipples. I have several lined up. When I ask you a question, you make sure you answer honestly." He warned.

"Yes, Sir," I whispered.

"Oh and one more thing. You are NOT allowed to cum until I allow it. Is that understood?"

"Yes, Sir," I whimpered now.

I was already dripping with excitement and now I wasn't allowed to cum. I had no clue how to stop an orgasm. Whenever I had one it just happened.

"Let's start with the pussy lips."

I heard the smirk in his voice and blushed, knowing he'd be looking right into my center. I felt a puff of air and damn if I my clit didn't tighten even more. I didn't cum but it was close. The next feeling took all thoughts of orgasm away. He'd attached two metal clamps to my pussy lips. Two on each side. The pain was excruciating.

"Painful?" he asked.

I was so confused by the pain, I yelled, "Take them off, Oh Dear god, please take them off."

Quick as lightning he took off all four but what followed wasn't relief, it was a rush of blood going through my nether lips that was just as painful as the clamps.

"Sh, wait it out, it will stop any moment now," Sir assured me while stroking my hair. "No clamps on your pussy lips, I guess?"

I was sweating and breathing fast and couldn't speak.

"Easy, now. Deep breaths. Do you want to be released?"

I let my breath out in a whoosh. As suddenly as the pain had started it was now only a light throbbing.

"No, Sir." I shook my head.

"Since these were the lightest clamps, I'm presuming that we can cross that off our list. Let's try your nipples, shall we?"

I felt his fingers on my nipples teasing them. Then his mouth covered them and sucked both nipples into point after which he blew on them, making them tighten up even more. When I felt a pinch as he attached a clamp onto my left nipple, it was unpleasant but not really painful. The other one was a bit more sensitive. I was breathing through my nose and with each breath my chest and therefore breasts moved.

"Let's see what your limit is, shall we?"

And before I could nod or say anything, he tightened the clamps. First one then the other. I started hyperventilating. It wasn't that it was as excruciating as the ones on my pussy but the feeling was so intense, it was like nothing I'd ever experienced before.

"Okay, I'm going to take them off now. It's going to hurt the same as when I removed the clamps from your pussy. Ready?"

Again he didn't wait for an answer, he just did it. This time I screamed bloody murder as the blood rushed to my poor nipples. I felt something else as the pulsing slowed. A finger was turning circles around my clit and tapping the butt plug. My scream turned into a long stretched out moan.

"Please,.." I begged.

"Please, what?"

"Please, may I cum, Sir?"

"No," his voice was gruff but instead of easing up on me he moved faster on my clit and the tapping.

"Oh, god, I'm going to cum."

I shook my head from left to right and tried to move my hips away from the temptation. His heavy hand pushed down on my stomach keeping my body still. His tongue descended on my clit and just as I was about to come completely undone, he stopped.

"Good girl," his voice rumbled into my pussy. He wasn't even touching it when I came. I tried to hide it but the uncontrollable movement of my hips and low throaty sound I couldn't keep in, betrayed me.

"Oops! Bad girl. I guess."

There wasn't malice in his voice or anything, rather satisfaction. He open handed slapped my pussy, making me cum again.

"And that was the last chance you had of choosing the part of your body that will be subjected to a tool of my own choosing. Lot's for you to think about during dinner, which I believe is ready." I wanted to growl at his pleased tone of voice. He'd done this all on purpose. I never stood a chance.

He undid the cuffs and the bindings around my thighs, before helping me up and taking the blindfold off. Taking my head between his hands we looked deep into each others' eyes. There was a certain tentative connection there, before he kissed me on the forehead and told me to put on the robe to have dinner.

"What about the butt plug, Sir?"

I slipped off the table a bit awkwardly.

"What about it?" he answered without turning around.

I sighed. Guess that meant I was keeping it in. This should be interesting.

Dinner was uneventful, except for the fact that I was sitting on a very sensitive pussy and a butt plug, covered only by a silk robe, which touched and teased my uber sensitive nipples the whole time. At least this time I was sitting on a softer, more comfortable chair.

Even though the food was delicious I couldn't really focus on what it was I was eating. I didn't drink any wine as Sir told me to hydrate with water. He did promise I could have wine or something stronger after my punishment.

"Ready for round two?" Sir asked after wiping his mouth with his napkin, trying but failing to hide his grin.

"Yes, Sir." I grabbed the table gathering all my courage on a deep breath

"Okay then, follow me." He was out the door by the time I pushed my chair away from the table.

It surprised me that walking became less awkward the longer I had the plug in.

Chapter Twenty three

We entered the Dungeon in silence. Sir disrobed me and fit the cuffs back on my wrists. We shared an intense look before he blindfolded me with a thick, black leather eye mask that he tightened around my head like a belt.

Taking my hand and an elbow, he guided me to the plush carpet that I knew by now was the center 'stage' of the room.

He lifted my hands high over my head, I heard a click. Once he let go, I noticed that my cuffs were connected to something making it impossible for me to do anything but hang. I realized it must be the hook in the ceiling. To relieve a bit of pressure from my wrists, I stood on my tip toes.

At first the twack sound didn't register until I felt the sting on my ass that followed it.

"Count and say 'thank you Sir.'"

"One, t-t-thank you Sir." Myind was still paying catch up.

The next hit was right underneath my buttocks and hurt like a mother fucker.

"Two," I shouted, followed by a quieter, "Thank you, Sir."

He hit me on each of my ass cheeks. I clenched them around the butt plug I'd almost forgotten.

The impact felt different, larger than the first two and I wondered if it was a different kind of tool he used. My ass started to heat up and I was hopping all over the place. It was hell not knowing where or when the next impact would come.

The next two hit me square on the nipple. A choked sound came from me, my scream stuck in my throat by the quick succession of slaps. It wasn't something thin, but flat, that was hitting my still sensitive nipples.

"Six, thank you, Sir!" I gasped.

"Four more to go. I'm going to take the blindfold off and let you choose the next tool and place, ok?" His tongue licked my left ear, making me shiver.

"Yes, Sir, thank you Sir," the answer tumbling from my lips in relief.

The eye mask came off and I was momentarily blinded. It wasn't that the room was bright, but coming out of the total darkness of the mask took a moment for my vision to adjust.

The first thing that came into focus was the table I'd been on earlier. It was filled to the brim with every type of whip, cane and other instruments I didn't recognize.

"You've had the pleasure of feeling the cane and the paddle on your ass. On your nipples I used the riding crop."

He showed them to me and I almost laughed out loud when I saw that the riding crop had a little hand as a tip.

"I would like to try the flogger next."

He put the riding crop on the table and lifted a heavy looking stocky handle. When it came off the table I saw it had lots of different straps attached to the handle. He came closer and caressed my legs, my pussy and breasts with the straps. I let my head fall back and moaned. One drop of moisture slipped out of my pussy and started it's way to the carpet down my leg.

"Yes, Sir." I whispered. I wanted it and knew exactly where I wanted it.

"Two on my ass and two on my breasts, if it pleases you, Sir." My eyes were hooded when I gazed at him.

"Kitten, you are gorgeous, all flushed from whipping and desire." He came closer, grabbed my neck with one hand and licked my ear, before whispering: "For once, your wish, is my command."

Letting go, he moved behind me. The flogger connected with my upper back and my whole bottom. He literally hit the wind out of me. My breath exited with a whoosh. He waited a bit but I couldn't pronounce any words. It was as if the heat from my ass was spreading to my inner core. When he hit next, I came undone, screaming like a banshee. I'd never in my life cum that hard and I passed out.

"Hey, kitten, wake up."

Slowly I became aware of a hand caressing my cheek and snuggled my face in it. The chuckle rumbling through the chest I was lying against made me purr.

"Kitten was the right pet name for you, huh?" Sir laughed, waking me up completely.

My face heated up. Remembering that I'd passed out was so embarrassing.

"You did well. I'm proud of you." His voice was deep with emotion which I couldn't decipher. "But I still need my last two strikes."

For some stupid reason I was near tears. I could feel them pricking in the corners of my eyes.

"I'm glad you came while being hit with my favourite flogger. I'm proud of you, Kitten. There's no need for tears. You'll still get those last two on your breasts, but not today. I think it would be best if you went to bed now." He gently wiped the tears from my cheeks.

"You're not disappointed?" I asked.

"No, I'm very pleased. I think we're going to be very compatible. We'll do a few more sessions, just to be sure."

He kissed me on the lips ever so sweetly and stood up to leave.

"Have a good night's sleep, I'll be expecting you at breakfast same as today." He winked and the light turned off. That's when I realised that

I was in my room, in my comfortable bed. Snuggling deeper under the covers I fell into a deep satisfied sleep with a smile on my face.

92

Chapter Twenty four

Daylight was streaming across my bed but I didn't want to wake up. Stretching, I yawned and then snuggled into the pillow again, until my alarm sounded for the third time. It really was time to drag myself out of my deliciously soft bed.

A quick shower later, I walked fully naked to the kitchen, more comfortable with it than I had been yesterday. Next to Sir's chair I kneeled into the bracelette position and waited.

When his chair scraped over the floor I didn't look up. I could see his feet positioned on either side of my knees.

"Good morning, Kitten. I need a good blow job before breakfast."

Without another word my hands went to his belt. Once I opened his trousers I smiled. He went commando. His cock sprang forward and I held it in my hand. Scooting a bit closer, I licked the pre-cum off and savoured it on my tongue.

I swirled my tongue around the head of his cock before wetting my lips and taking him as deep as I could.

"Hands behind your back."

I did as told and soon knew why. He put his hands on my head and grabbed my hair. His hips surged up and with fast thrusts, he teased my gag reflex. I had to clasp my hands together behind my back to prevent myself to push him away.

Drool was streaming from the corners of my mouth and my eyes teared up. I kept gagging and it seemed to turn him on even more. When I thought I would throw up he stopped and came in my mouth.

I was breathing heavily through my nose but licked him clean. With a nod, he put himself away and went back to his coffee and newspaper.

I wiped my cheeks and mouth and sat down to eat my breakfast. Naked. It wasn't until I was almost done that I realized there was a cushion on my seat so my bruised bum could have a break. That small consideration made me smile.

The rest of the day went as the day before, except for now I'd decided to wear no underwear and it was both a relief and felt a bit naughty. I had a smile on my face the whole day and couldn't wait until evening.

"Greta, we're going to have an early dinner in two hours and start after that." Sir said without looking up from his computer. He excused me to my room.

It was four PM so I took a bath. The soak did wonders for both my sore muscles and the stripes I received. I didn't dare chase an orgasm as I was pretty sure that wasn't something that was allowed. Instead I rubbed a soothing lotion over my body and dressed in a lovely cream colored dress with pink four inch heels for dinner. All these beautiful clothes should be worn. I left off the panties. I was quite sure I wouldn't need them.

Dinner was delicious as usual and we talked about the work that had been done that day and the work that needed to be done tomorrow. Before I knew it he shoved back his chair.

"Come along, kitten, let's go to the Dungeon." He held out his hand and grinning like a fool, I took it. The maid came in and started clearing the table, while we left.

"Undress and stand against the cross," he ordered the moment we arrived at the bottom of the stairs.

I kicked off the heels and pulled the dress over my head, tossing it to the side. Naked I stood against the cross with my back. Sir moved closer and I saw the leather cuffs. He put one on each ankle and each wrist. Pinching a nipple playfully in between. When he was finished he pressed his chest against mine, his hand moving down to my pussy.

"Today we're going to check your flogging boundaries. Remember your safeword?" His voice whispered in my ear, I could only nod, which earned me an open handed slap on my pussy.

"Yes, Sir!" I shouted.

His fingers moved my pussy lips aside and he dipped the tip of his finger in my juices before zeroing in on my clit and circling it lazily. His hot breath was in my neck now, when he bit down, I moaned. I loved being bitten in the neck. He softened the bite by licking it. His pace on my clit went faster and I couldn't hold back the whimper escaping my mouth. I was very close and started moving my hips. I wanted his finger there, no, his cock. I needed it. Yesterday he had denied me that pleasure and today I hungered for it. Having him cum in my mouth was good but not good enough.

When my thighs started shaking announcing the beginning of my orgasm he stepped away. A whine came from my throat. A sound I'd never made before.

"Turn around and reach for the tips of the cross with your hands and spread your legs."

Pouting, I did as I was told. A smack to my ass was his answer to my pout.

"If you're a good girl, you'll get all the orgasms I can wring out of you."

His entire body pressed into my back while he attached the cuffs to each part of the cross. With my legs spread, my pussy lips opened up and I felt the cool air caressing my wet opening.

First he let the flogger fall lightly onto my back, more like a caress. The leather straps stroked me from shoulders to ass. I wriggled my ass. Not that I could move it much, but it elicited a chuckle from Sir and that had been my point.

"Teasing slut," his baritone voice rumbled.

The light patting of the flogger turned up in force. He slowly built up the pace and the impact. I was relishing the fact that I'd been able to keep quiet for at least a minute but then I started moaning. He went up a notch with the force of his flogging and my moans turned into screeches. He increased his force again and this time the impact threw me against the cross. I couldn't keep the screams and groans from echoing around the empty dungeon. Just when I thought I was going to have to use my safe-word he slowed down.

When I sagged into the cross, he built up to the screaming stage and as before the moment I got close to shouting my safe-word, he eased off again. Once my mind made this connection, I let go. When he went harder, I didn't scream anymore, I moaned and was in heaven. I felt the impact but it felt so good. I was spacing out and when he hit my pussy, I woke up out of my daze. He kept going but at a much slower pace, the hits not as hard and finally he stopped.

Releasing me from the cross and he laid me down on the soft carpet. Grabbing my useless legs he lifted them over his shoulders and slammed his cock in my soaking wet pussy. I spasmed around him as I came immediately on a long drawn out moan. He kept pounding until he stopped buried deep inside. He threw his head back and the pulsing of his cock against my inner walls pulled another orgasm from my tired body, clamping down hard on his cock. He groaned and reached his own orgasm with a deep groan.

We stayed on the carpet, both catching our breaths. He kept his weight off of me with his hands next to my head.

"I think we'll leave all the orgasms you can take for tomorrow," Sir said with an arched eyebrow.

"I believe that's a good idea, Sir. I think I've reached my limit for tonight."

"You even went into subspace," he sounded surprised. I had read something about that when I was checking the internet about BDSM on my phone over lunch.

It's literally when you space out and can take any pain.

"Did you slip into Domspace?" I wondered since it wasn't easy for a Dom. He had to take responsibility all the time, after all.

"I was in there for a second with you and that has never happened before," he admitted, now leaning on his forearms, kissing my nose.

"How do you feel?" he asked.

"Well and truly spent and satisfied." I grinned at him.

"I'm glad, because this was one of the best experiences for me and I've been doing this for quite some time."

I grabbed his head and pulled it down for a deep kiss. We cuddled a little bit longer before calling it a night and going to our respective bedrooms. I wasn't sure why we didn't sleep together but I had an inkling that it had something to do with the collaring. I missed him.

Chapter Twenty five

After the day's work, Sir decided to have a late dinner so we could do the edging play first. I was sweating, swearing and eventually crying and begging. When he gave in, I had an orgasm that was more intense than any I've had before. Was it worth it? I didn't know.

He kept true to his word about making me orgasm all evening the next day. Each time I turned into a lump noodle, thinking I couldn't come anymore, he wrung another one out of my tired body. In the end he fucked me, but I couldn't come anymore, which had been frustrating.

The next evening had me lying on the table with my hands cuffed to my ankles again. He sat next to me with a wide smile on his face while I sweated up a storm.

A fucking machine installed at the end of the table thrusted at a maddeningly slow pace in and out of me. With a magic wand he worked my clit. I'd been close to orgasm four times already. My thighs were quivering, my stomach muscles tensing up everytime. I couldn't hide the signals and he was reading my body like a book.

He took the wand away again and turned it off.

"I believe you still owe me two strikes, my little slut." He said with a glint in his eyes.

The riding crop appeared out of nowhere and I felt it land on my clit. I didn't realise that he left the crop there until he started lightly tapping it on my clit. He stood next to the fucking machine and turned up the speed. The thing was pumping at a deliciously fast pace and with the same pace he tapped the riding crop.

"You look fucking beautiful." I heard him murmur in awe.

"Oh, yes, Sir, please can I cum?" I was very close.

"No," he answered and stopped everything.

He moved the fucking machine aside, undid my cuffs and lifted me off the table. He then draped me over it with the tips of my toes barely touching the ground. By the time I got a grip on the table he slammed into me and his balls slapped against my clit. He grabbed my hair making me arch my back.

"I love the way you can take all of me and still feel as tight as the first time," he groaned. I started pulsing around him.

"Don't!" he ordered.

I could barely hold back. Tears of frustration were now running down my cheeks.

"And I definitely love it when you cry out of frustration. My little pain slut."

"My...good...girl," he said each word followed by a hard thrust. "Now!"

The word was enough to make me come. He let go of my hair to hold on to my hips as he came undone as well, forcing another orgasm from my body

This time I didn't pass out but the orgasms were intensely mind blowing after being on edge for two hours. When I could breathe normally again he surprised me.

"Shall we take a shower?"

I looked up at him in surprise and there was a gentleness about him I'd only noticed when he kissed me before bed.

"Yes, Sir," I said.

"Get that sweet ass of yours moving." he said jokingly and slapped me, eliciting a squeak.

"Which way, Sir?" I asked once we exited the Dungeon.

"Follow me." He took my hand and we walked in the opposite direction of my room.

When we entered the room I was hit by deja-vu. This room was exactly like mine, except for the colors. Everything was black, even the curtains. When he opened the bathroom door I was almost blinded by the white, it was such a contrast. The tub was the same size as mine, but the shower could fit four people.

While I'd been admiring the bathroom, he'd taken his clothes off. Closing in behind me, his cock pushed into the small of my back. His hands moved to my arms and lifted them to drape them behind his head. Stroking back down my arms he caressed my breasts bringing my nipples to attention. He filled his hands with my breasts and squeezed them firmly.

"Mmm," was all I said and closed my eyes.

One hand made its way to my pussy and opened my lips while his teeth nipped my neck. My body pulsed with the attention. One finger slipped inside my still wet pussy and I widened my stance to give him more access. He thrust a second finger in and started scissoring them until he found the spot he was looking for. He pushed my G spot with both fingers and bit my neck bringing me over the edge with little difficulty. Thankfully he had one arm under my breasts because my legs gave out. I wasn't sure how many orgasms I'd had that evening and still he managed to wring one out of me.

"Shower," he whispered in my ear.

"Sure," I breathed back, earning me another slap on my ass.

I giggled and walked over to the glass doors. He was right behind me and turned on the taps. Sprays hit me from above and the front and took my breath away with the freezing cold water.

"Bloody hell." I gasped for air.

The water was now turning a steamy hot temperature and I sighed in bliss.

"You were hiding behind me!" I finally realised.

"That's what you get for being a naughty minx."

He didn't let me turn around, but lifted one of my legs and put it on a little stool that was positioned to the right. Lifting me by the hips he penetrated me from behind.

"Come for me again," he commanded.

"I don't know if I can, Sir." I admitted reluctantly.

"I'm sure you can," he said with his fingers already zeroed in on my clit and sure enough I felt an orgasm building.

He took his finger away and turned me around. Pushing me against the wall opposite of the sprays, he kissed me hard, our tongues battling, his cock pressing into my stomach.

"Wrap your legs around my waist." He nibbled my lower lip.

It wasn't a request but an order and I didn't hesitate to follow. His strong hands wrapped around my ass. He squeezed and lifted me off my feet. I wrapped my arms around his neck and my legs around his waist. His cock slid home, right where it belonged, in my wet pussy. He thrust into me, my back slamming into the wall with the force. He wasn't holding back and with his pubic hair tickling my clit my legs started to quiver.

"I'm gonna come," I gasped in disbelief.

"Yes, kitten, come for me," he growled out and pounded even faster.

When I came undone again, he growled even louder and shouted my name. My real name, Greta, came from this man's lips. My vagina muscles were milking his cock and the tiniest bit that he could move brought on another aftershock orgasm.

At that moment I knew. I was in love with this amazing man, my boss, my Master, my Dom.

We finished our shower and I tiptoed into his room wrapped in a bathrobe that was two sizes too big.

"Oh, my, God!" I blushed bright red.

"What?" Sir's head came from around the bathroom door.

"Someone was here, while we were..." I waved my hand between us.

"Yes, so?" He frowned.

There was a small round table at the foot end of the bed that hadn't been there before. A bouquet of red roses sat in the middle, next to a large candelabra. A cart carried plates covered in cloches to keep the food warm. On one side of the table was a beautifully wrapped white box. It was so out of place in the black room that it caught my eye immediately.

I felt arms wrapping me from behind.

"You like?"

"Yes, but what must they have thought?"

"That we were both very satisfied after a workout," he chuckled.

I slapped him on his arm, giggling but still embarrassed.

"I guess they're used to it," I mused.

There was silence behind me and his arms wrapped me tighter in the hug.

"You're the first woman to stay in this house, let alone this room, for the past twenty years. That's how long I've been searching for the perfect partner." His voice was rough with emotion. "Open your present, kitten."

He gently ushered me forward. He puttel out the chair, I sat down and he pushed it closer to the table. With his hands on my shoulders, I looked at the satin red bow wrapped around the white box.

"Go on," he urged.

I took a deep breath and undid the bow. With a click I opened the box and inside on a silk white bed was the most beautiful collar I'd even seen. It was satin and deep red. There was a black clasp in the back and a ring in the front. The ring sparkled like a proper diamond.

"It's beautiful," I choked out. It was the most meaningful gift I'd ever received.

"Greta, my kitten, will you be my sub and partner for life?"

I looked to my left and saw Sir on one knee.

"YES!" I screamed, "Yes, Sir." I added.

"Give me the collar so I can put it on."

When I gave it to him I frowned when he took the ring off the collar.

"In public you can wear the ring as a regular ring," he held out his hand for mine and slid it on.

"In private, you can pull your collar through it." He took the ring off my finger and slid the velvet choker through the ring. I held my hair up so he could put it around my neck and clasp it in the back.

"Now this is mine and you can only take it off when I want you too." He held up a little silver key. The key that locked me as his sub and fiancée.

With tears streaming down my cheeks, I threw myself against him.

"I love you, Sir," I whispered in his neck.

"And I love you, my kitten." His voice was muffled by my hair. I pulled back and held his face between my hands. Our gazes locked. I took the initiative and kneeled in front of him, tugging on his hair to pull him closer for a kiss that made my toes curl and my pussy wet.

§§§

Author's note:

I hope you all enjoyed reading this story as much as I've enjoyed writing it. Please don't hesitate to leave a review!

A tiny bit of feedback in regards to BDSM:

You might have noticed that Sir gives Greta quite a bit of information not only about the action but also afterwards.

Not everyone is aware that after care is just as important in the BDSM world as impact play, rope play, shibari, etc. It is the essential bonding and emotional support towards one another. Powerful emotions can occur between partners sometimes even sub- or Dom space.

Just make sure that you all take care of each other in the same way Greg took care of his sub but also the same way that his subs hugs take care of his personal needs. Everyone is different, respect that and respect each other!

Sometimes a collar is seen in the BDSM world as an engagement or even in some circles a wedding ring.

There are several ways to experience BDSM. Greta and her Boss do scenes and in the privacy of their Dungeon or bedroom.

Other people experience BDSM as 24/7. This means that all day every day they interact as slave/Master or Mistress or Dom/me/sub.

The scenes I described here in this series are only a tip of the iceberg. There are lots of different ways to enjoy BDSM. Kinks are different for everyone and finding that one person that has the same kinks and same feelings with certain tools, actions, is not easy.

I hope you enjoyed my book.

My contact details are below, if you're interested in more books, my newsletter or updates.

As with every author, I love feedback and will love you forever if you leave a review.

I wish you health and happiness!

Love,

Tiny

Thank you for reading
About the Author

TINY SPARKS IS THE nom de plume of an author of erotica and erotic romance short stories.

Her husband and their special relationship are the inspiration for most of her erotic short stories. She is his submissive and therefore has experience in the BDSM scene.

When she could not find enough stories to satisfy her, she decided to write her own.

Some stories offer sexy fantasies with a personal knowledge of the BDSM world. Others' are more in the paranormal or fantasy genre.

SUBSCRIBE TO MY NEWSLETTER to be kept up to date on all things books, BDSM and so much more! 'Tiny's First Spark' is an exclusive story only acquired by subscribing. The story of my introduction into BDSM and meeting my husband is Tiny's First Spark.

Once a week you'll receive promotions, updates on future books and reviews of books I read and recommend.

Newsletter: https://landing.mailerlite.com/webforms/landing/f7o1s4

WEBSITE: http://www.tinysparksx.wixsite.com/tinysparks

Facebook: http://www.facebook.com/tinysparksx
Twitter: http://www.twitter.com/SparksxTiny
Instagram: http://www.instagram.com/sparksxtiny
Goodreads: http://www.goodreads.com/tiny_sparksx

Other books by Tiny Sparks

BDSM Erotic Stories: https://books2read.com/u/38yPZ7

1. INITITATION https://books2read.com/u/4ApZnJ
2. Introduction https://books2read.com/u/3n5Oeo
3. Invitation https://books2read.com/u/bzZ5QD
4. Inspiration https://books2read.com/u/4A52ao

TINA'S STORY 1-4 (COMPLETE sereies of BDSM Erotic Stories) https://books2read.com/u/38yPZ7
Lesbian Erotica:
The Office Party https://books2read.com/u/mZZMDD

GENERAL EROTICA:
The Mansion https://books2read.com/u/mYyBBY
The Escort https://books2read.com/u/b5X6Yk

VAMPIRE EROTICA:
The Ball https://books2read.com/u/bwo09a
The Cave https://books2read.com/u/3k5JQ8
Millennial Ball https://books2read.com/u/4joOwl

WEREWOLF EROTICA:
   Riding Red https://books2read.com/u/38yaja

BDSM EROTIC STORIES
   Initiation BDSM Erotic Stories
   Book 1 in the BDSM Erotic Stories Series

Tina has a fabulous imagination, giving her the opportunity to write sexy articles for a magazine. When offered a full time writer's gig, she's all for it. This time, however, her imagination won't help her as they want a personal touch. A colleague at her current job might just give her all the experience she needs, and more. How far will she go to become a full time writer?

https://books2read.com/u/4ApZnJ

The whole series is now available as Tina's Story 1-4 BDSM Erotic Stories

https://books2read.com/u/38yPZ7